WATERMAN'S FIRE

By

ANGELA NOWAK

DEDICATION

To Lizzie, Elijah and Daniel

Waterman's Fire, A Novel

All scripture references are taken from ESV

e-mail address: angelanowak127@gmail.com

Also by A. Nowak:

Big and Brave

CONTENTS

PART ONE:

WAVE RIDER

A waterman is a person—surfer, diver, windsurfer, paddle-boarder, who dedicates the majority of his life to the ocean.

1

The man's lifeless face was eerie. James had never witnessed anyone die before. What was he doing swimming on a day like this? Spectators were pulled in together by the accident. Suddenly this became the business of everybody who was on the beach.

"If he's not conscious, the chances are slim. Timing is everything."

"Need to watch out for the undertows…"

James caught the trail of the conversations around him. Standing around powerlessly, a fast-gathering crowd came up with various explanations.

Earlier, James had pleaded with his mother to drive him down to the coast. The day seemed promising: sunny, not too much wind, a perfect day for paddle-boarding, if you ask. A sports-minded introvert, all he was keen about was biking, paddle-boarding or swimming. His new paddleboard was a modern technology masterpiece; he could not wait to test it out. James blew all his birthday money and more to buy the Aquamarina SPK-1, but it was worth every penny. His mum's car didn't have a roof rack, so now he could just inflate it whilst on the beach. What an ingenious idea! If ever James happened to meet the person behind this design, he would give him a massive hug. Also, according to the description, the board was a Ferrari on the water!

"Look, the sea is so choppy!" James threw his hands up in the air.

There was plenty of parking along Felixstowe beach. The wind was blowing steadily, creating small, but fast coming waves. Once again the weather forecast didn't deliver! The sun was super dazzling though, creating silvery sparkles on the water surface.

"Oh, well, we can't order the weather!" Leila, his mother, stated the obvious.

"I was so looking forward to testing out the paddle board!" James muttered, unreconciled with the situation.

"Sun's still out. There is plenty of fresh air. It could be raining...."

When did his mother suddenly became such an optimist? He wondered.

James figured it made sense to stay for a while since they had driven all this way. Somehow the sea always drew him in, evoking a sense of pure awe in him with its salty air and hidden, unmeasured power. He stared at the endless stretch of shimmering water as seagulls cruised above, confirming such a thought by its gleeful screeching.

As soon as they parked, grey clouds began to gather and the wind picked up speed, blowing anyone on the Suffolk coast back into their cars. James was still unpacking when the accident happened.

"There is someone struggling out there!" The life guards were on full alert already. As it turned out, a man was being pulled by the tide out into the sea. In theory, James realized that people died all the time, but seeing that man losing his battle with life, made it more real than all the news he had ever watched. A fit and healthy teen, he hadn't particularly considered the subject of dying.

The Felixstowe life guards were doing their best to save the man. One was pulling out the boat, while the other grabbed the lifesaving ring. They were struggling against the waves; the ambulance helicopter was on its way. At last, the man was pulled out. The gathered crowd cheered in relief, but in spite of the joint efforts of life guards and promptly arriving paramedics who gave CPR, the verdict was cruel: "Dead." Dark green, slimy seaweed got tangled in his hair, as a cruel warning to anyone daring to challenge the sea. The Paramedics promptly carried the man away on a stretcher. A different feeling, like the change in the weather, enveloped the crowd, now totally silent. Burdened by such sudden turn of events, everyone began to disperse, leaving the beach to the seagulls.

"Let's go, darling," at last Leila pulled her son on his sleeve.

"Nothing could be done, man! The undercurrent is so strong here. Even an Olympic swimmer would have struggled. I wonder if he was thinking straight?" One of the life guards reasoned out loud. Both Leila and James nodded back in agreement. James had never felt more powerless, seeing a grip of death that close up, he knew now it was outside of a human control.

"Let's go." James zipped his jacket, pulling his hood tighter. The sun, playing hide and seek, disappeared again behind the clouds. The wind, still strong, pushed its unwelcomed chill right through his coat. Somehow, witnessing a life snatched by his much-loved sea so cruelly, made James also think of his father. He was the first to encourage the love of water in him. They'd spent endless hours at the coast together, his father being a keen surfer.

Just like now, in one fateful day, a dramatic change in his life took place.

"James, I'm going away," his father unexpectedly broke out.

James knew now that nothing, absolutely nothing, could have prepared him for that moment. The news was unexpected, breaking out as a storm on a tranquil day.

"Where are you going?" James asked, scared to hear the answer. His father's voice, sounding fake, confirmed his fears.

"I want to travel, explore some surfing first in Australia, then in Mexico. You know… while I still have the energy to do it."

"What about us? Are you just going to take off?" Angry, James still tried to reason with him. An unwelcome, but powerful intruder pushed in by its sheer strength, while they spoke.

"You need to carry on with your education! Your mother is here for you. And before you know it, I'll be back." This promise sounded hollow, feeding the fire of anger that started to burn inside. James wanted to break something violently, releasing it out. *If you want to play that game, I will never speak to you again*, thought James.

Now, whilst looking at the dead man, the tragic scene triggered the memory of their last conversation. James refused to say goodbye then. His father's promise to come back was like the seaweed to the dead man, still tangled in his hair, useless. The anger turning into hate, entered as a stranger, but became a permanent lodger now.

One thing was a bit of a surprise: even though, first shaken by the accident and then, by the crashing waves of vicious memory, his desire to live on the edge didn't shift.

The recklessness that drove him towards the sense of feeling immortal, stayed. Was it out of stubbornness towards his father's decision to quit on him? Or was he simply wired this way? Often James wished that his mother shared his passion for water sport. At times he needed her to be just like his father, especially with the coming holiday in Dorset. In reality, she was a typical female: overcautious, protective and worried plenty. James knew that such thoughts sounded mean even if he had a good reason to think it. At times, an irritation rose inside of him because they didn't see eye to eye; her pestering him with criticism when he wanted a chilled-out parent!

Leila tried to alleviate the situation, the drive back purposefully cheered up by the loud tunes on the radio. But the songs couldn't stop James from his thoughts. For the past few years James had tried to forget about his dad. He had not spoken to him in three years, but time didn't seem to make his feelings less acute. Instead, his anger still dominated all other emotions. The summer break didn't sound promising either. He was in the soup, so much so, he decided to use his last desperate option. Prayer! James hadn't spoken to God either since he had entered his teens. But today, he somehow felt different about it, realizing that both he and the dead man on the beach had something in common. James simply couldn't rescue his situation himself.

"God, please let this summer break not be ruined! Can my mother, for once, not worry about me all the time? I guess… I will try to talk to You more often."

James continued in thoughtful, quiet mood till they got home. Hiding in his room was best. Leila got busy in the kitchen.

"Dinner is on the table. Hurry up, I'm famished!" Leila's melodious voice urged half an hour later, returning James to reality. Rushing downstairs as the hunger got the better off him, he suddenly felt convicted of his attitude. His life wasn't a bad life, but something was amiss, he figured this much. Lanky and still growing, he was constantly hungry. Most of his friends from school had bigger families. He envied them, but not the size of their dinner portions!

"This looks all right, mum!"

"Tuck in." Leila blessed the food, but thanking God for it.

Leila and James were complete opposites. Singing was breathing to her. Leila found great pleasure in it, whilst adventurous sports made her nervous. Being at work in the office all day, then training her voice in her spare time, she didn't possess agility of youth. She didn't train her muscles for hours, like her son. Being healthy, able to look after her son, it was all that mattered to her. And she was appreciated her thick, chestnut hair, something she could show off. James couldn't imagine even listening to opera. Ever. Deep down he knew his mother tried her best to raise him. The difference of opinion between them could not be put down to him "being a teenager" as some of her friends suggested. *Was she ever a teen herself?* This was a real puzzle to him. Often James felt lonely and not understood. At one point, James considered making friends with the lads from his mother's church, but they were a bit older, and being on the shy side wasn't to his advantage.

"Aren't you hungry?" Leila urged, looking keenly at her tall, fast-growing lad.

"Ok, mum, don't fuss." James replied. Don't be desperate, a teenagers' unwritten rule was glue, stuck in his mind. He could not easily shake it off even when he wasn't around his friends.

"Are you excited about our trip to Dorset? I just got a confirmation e-mail saying that the cottage is reserved for the next week to Mrs. Leila Orwell. How about that?"

"I was, but not now, to be honest..." James began. "You've probably already lined up garden centres or concerts to attend. Especially now, since that man on the beach... You know that all I want is to spend every minute in the sea," he avidly backed up his obsession for sports.

"Yes, I do. I'm not planning on caging you! This is your holiday to enjoy. James, you are growing up so fast, but I will always be a hovering hen. Can't help it. It's a mother's instinct." Leila needed him to understand.

Enjoying the pasta with pesto dish, as his appetite kicked in, James wisely decided to drop the matter. At least he secured some ground with her. As long as he was left out of the usual cultural experience ordeal, he would be happy. Arguing further before the trip was unfair.

" Will you come with me to church on Sunday?"she asked in hope.

"When I'm ready for it, mum," James stated. He would be the laughing stock of the school, a Bible basher. No, thank you. Maybe that is why he stopped praying, taking his frustration into sport, gaining some control in his life. The last thing he needed was for his friends to mock him. James knew he was performing well, excelling in different sports. At the same time, he knew the feeling driving him was unhealthy, like doping. Brushing such a depressing revelation off like an annoying cobweb, James decided to catch up with Phil, his mate from school, before heading on holiday first thing tomorrow.

Leila wiped a tear. And why even bother with makeup remover? Surely tears were natural and free. She whispered in good faith: "Lord, you have to do it. Please convince James of your truth. Convict him that today is the day of salvation!"

In the morning, everything was already packed neatly in their small, but reliable bottle green Volkswagen. His mother was super organized.

"Are you ready? Lots of miles to cover today!"

While pondering the prospect of a long drive to Dorset, Leila came up with a plan to stop and visit her old school friend.

"Why don't we stop in Brighton to see Maggie? A bit out of our way, but Brighton on sea is a good plan, isn't it?" James didn't mind as long as the words "beach" or "sea" were mentioned.

"Cool by me," James shouted through the half open door.

Leila Facetimed with Maggie, telling her when to expect them. James recalled that Maggie was a committed vegan. He loved her chilled fruity desserts when the weather was especially hot.

"Maggie is thrilled about it." Leila delivered her news. "She is pioneering a new raw chocolate bar as we speak. Releases lots of energy, according to her."

"Can't wait to try it!" James, for an odd reason, always felt more comfortable around older folk. As a rule, talking to someone his age was a true effort.

After a couple of stops at the services and hours of driving, a sign of colourful flowers greeted: "Welcome to

Brighton." The journey towards pleasant past-time flew by. The minute Maggie and Leila saw each other, still standing outside a red brick house, they were acting like a couple of school girls. James was pleased that no one knew him around here. Andrew, Maggie's husband, was at home. Nothing made James happier than the offer to walk to the beachfront. After a long drive in the heat, cooling down with the fruit sorbet, James was more than ready to head out again.

"Do you mind if we take the dogs?" Two young Dalmatians with brown spots were wiggling their tails in anticipation.

"Not at all." James couldn't take his eyes of those beauties.

With the dogs leading the way, they took a narrow passageway down to the Brighton Pier. James studied Andrew for a moment, realizing that his solid build didn't happen on its own. There was something reliable about him. James could not help thinking that.

"They're very young. It's better we avoid the busy streets," explained Andrew. "So James, how did you get into paddle-boarding? Your mother says you would live in the water if you could."

"Dunno, really, just fell in love with it. I had a go at skateboarding. It was fun, but I found it too rough. Don't fancy injuries. I prefer to do water sports, even with the wind against me. And yourself?" Andrew was easy to talk to.

"I grew up near the coast, then ended up in the Royal Navy. Easy to love the sea, isn't it?"

James couldn't agree more.

"How was it… in the Navy, if you don't mind sharing?" James's interest was on the rise.

"Not what I expected. Scraping ice off the submarine isn't everyone's cup of tea, but it was character shaping. Made me tougher, with more endurance, if you like."

"Oh yeah," James nodded in agreement. There was something very captivating in Andrew's personality, no doubt.

"Sometimes sufferings and difficulties are the best tools in making us in who we really are. You know the type, like Job, from the Bible," clarified Andrew.

James just listened, not sure what to say to that.

"Oh. I paddle on my board even in winter," James wished to impress Andrew.

"How about a Boxing Day swim then? Perhaps you can come down again and spend Christmas with us!" Andrew offered mischievously. Then he threw a real challenge out. "No wet suits. Are you up for it?"

"What? That's mad! Have you done it before?"

"Every Boxing Day, without fail: it strengthens your immune system and it's good for the blood vessels. Didn't you know? It's tradition in the Navy."

"Impressive!"

"Does your mum approve of your water sport?" Andrew randomly asked.

"She's frightened of most adventurous things on land, let alone in the sea! Opera is more her forte." He spat his answer.

"I've heard her in a concert. She is really good, you know. Her voice has such strenght, reaching you deep inside." Andrew meant it. Sensing some hesitation, he quizzed further: "You don't approve?"

"Not my style." James rushed the answer.

"Hmmm, personally I don't divide music or singing into styles. Unusual you might think. . . . At least not since I was a teenager."

"So, how do you view music then? There are different styles to choose from, aren't there?" James didn't wish to play word games, wishing for a concrete answer.

"Of course, there is a personal preference in styles of music. I'm more interested in the music that we all make in life. Our actions and words, just like music, display what's in our hearts. What if everything that we did or said became music! How would your tune sound? Ever thought of that? Do you know what I mean? If we put the person before their talent, this way we can appreciate each other first of all. Then the styles lose predominance. Have whatever style you want, as long as there is an enjoyable sound of the heart."

"When you put it that way… I've never thought about in like that. In other words, you're saying that my mother is a kind, caring person, which shows in her actions so whatever style she sings in is awesome?" James unscramble the idea.

"Clever lad. Your teachers must be thrilled with you!" Andrew was pleased by such a conclusion. "It is that simple:

when you work it out, styles will be of no consequence," he shouted out, pulling the dogs back, which were only eager to run faster.

A range of emotions travelled James's face, a deeply thoughtful expression settling in. In one stride, they continued their walk along the beach. Andrew finally let the Dalmatians off the leash. An hour later, exhausted from such a fast pace, they headed back to the house, so James and Leila could continue their drive to Dorset.

"Such a pity we must drive on. The shortest visit ever! Will you come and see us in Poole?" suggested Leila.

"We will try our best." Maggie gladly accepted the offer.

James patted the dogs one last time. In return, they licked his fingers with vigour. Andrew gave him a strong embrace before parting.

"It was a real treat to spend some time. Take care."

"See you soon." Both Andrew and Maggie waved them off.

James sensed that something had melted inside of him. His mother was revving the gas pedal, eager to get on with the rest of their journey.

A detour from Suffolk to Brighton was a pleasant enough. As Leila pulled in front of the rented cottage, she gently tapped her son on the shoulder, trying to wake him up. The night already fell as a blanket.

"Ok, wake up sleepy! We made it. Time to stretch your legs!"

Sky reaching, slender pine trees and impressive size houses, as though in competition, were overlooking the cliffs; the sea was shimmering in the light of the moon below. A sense of peace washed over James as he was yawning, confirming that this holiday would be beyond his usually low expectations. Loaded with bags, he marched toward the cottage. *Why would he even think that?*

"Wow, check this place out!"

Somehow Poole felt like a different world.

"A friend from church warned me about breath-taking views! Admittedly, the beauty of the place surpasses my expectations." Leila broke out.

But James could not wait to check out the beach. He was sure his mother would insist on unpacking first.

To his surprise, as though reading his thoughts, Leila offered to walk down the Canford Cliff Promenade.

"Sure thing." James didn't need to be asked twice. Sleep was the last thing on his mind, now his anticipation growing of what lay ahead. Armed with flashlights, they walked.

Soon enough, standing high up on the top of the cliffs, t the panoramic view stretched in front of them in the moonlight: majestic pine trees behind and his much-loved, forever-stretching sea ahead.

2

The sun was forcefully pushing through the curtains, acting as an alarm. After glancing at the clock, James jumped out of bed, realizing how late it was. The quiet around here was unreal. Their cottage, surrounded by a pine trees forest, had only the birds nearby to make a pleasant racket. He hardly needed peace and quiet, unlike his mother who probably enjoyed such paradise. Fit to work for the weather forecast himself, James checked the Met Office daily. The weather in England was extremely unpredictable, always giving people an opportunity to complain; a classic British pastime. On holiday it had power to make or break James's plans. Eager to get out of the house, he was out of the door, with a banana between his teeth and a board in his arm. James sped away.

"Mother, meet you at the beach," he eventually shouted, already by the back gate.

Greeted by a cornflower-blue sky, with the air already warming, James could not wait to get to the beach.

He was rather pleased now that they had explored the place last night. Passing through the village, with a bakery showing off a row of delicious looking buns, the walk took him about ten minutes.

The turquoise sea, endlessly stretching was calm, with a few sail boats. The sun was blinding and the sand all evened out, ready for the next lot of tourists. A gentle breeze swept over his skin. The beach, perfect as it could be, beckoned him.

Swiftly blowing up the paddle board with an air pump, James, with a sense of utter pleasure, stepped into the refreshingly chilled water. There were two or three brave early risers out there in their wetsuits. It felt liberating to be doing what he loved so much; becoming one with nature where he didn't have to pretend or please anyone. His sole task was on conquering his fears. So what if he wasn't academic? If only his mother or his teachers experienced similar sense of freedom as he had in water, perhaps they would understand. His mother stressed out over his grades as if it were the end of the world! While in Brighton, Andrew caused him rethink his attitude a bit, but still James ached for activities that made him feel alive. He was not prepared to compromise on what was important to him. *Everyone can get lost with their strong opinions. This is my life to live, right?*

After a good paddle James was starving. The water felt fresh and invigorating. His wetsuit allowed him to spend as long as he wanted in the water, still feeling comfortable enough. But the hunger took over. His mother should be here by now.

"Hi, where are you?" James was pleased she answered her phone.

"Oh, I started to read and lost track of time," Leila explained.

"I'm starving!" Honesty prevailed since the holidays started; his friends' influence already grew faint. "Can you please bring a packed lunch to the beach?" James pleaded with hope.

"On my way!" Leila loved to provide good nutrition for her growing son.

If only we could agree so easily on everything! James felt so at ease when they agreed.

Waiting for the food, he thought of Andrew in particular. He hoped his mum's friends will join them here. Maggie's bars – he could murder one of Maggie's bars right now!

Looking around, James hoped to make friends with someone while in Dorset. However, the chance of that was zero to none. Then he recalled the peace that he felt yesterday. Will his prayer make a difference he wondered. His mother had an advantage in this area, he had to give her that; she read the Bible, went to the local church and always prayed. While lying on the sand, he kept watching the swimmers; two older men slowly passed up and down, a few kids splashing, but apart from that no one else was rushing to swim. He couldn't comprehend this. James complained to his mother that those who lived by the beach, but didn't obsess with it, didn't deserve the location! She only laughed at such vivid indignation.

"Here you go." A picnic basket landed right next to him.

"What express service! Thanks mum!"

Food always tasted better outdoors. He tucked in, what a spread it was: French stick, cheese, Spanish chorizo and olives.

"Will I be able to balance on my board afterwards?"

"I couldn't balance before lunch or after, if that's any consolation!" His mother's frankness was a true habit.

Riding the board demanded building up serious muscles, while displaying flawless coordination, it was true. James considered how friends often commented that Leila was perfectly built for singing. Her best friend Maggie had a valid point whenever she asked: "Have you ever seen a skinny opera singer?" She might be right, who knows. James's opinions were as malleable as clay, fuelled by his ever-changing convictions.

Even right after devouring all the food, James continued to paddle for hours. He believed that anyone could try anything if they could be bothered. He didn't rush to apply such theory to his learning though. Herein laid the friction between them; while Leila pushed him towards more studying, he wished her to appreciate his love for adventurous, sporty activities. At the same time, he believed that it was impossible to change anyone if they could not see it themselves. The million dollar question was who would change first? James sincerely wished that it would not have to be him.

"It's getting too hot. I'd better head back before I get sunburnt." Leila at last decided.

James promised not to stay for much longer himself.

After few hours, worn out for one day, James knew it was time to pack up.

Retracing the route he had taken hours earlier, James observed Sandbanks village with interest. A few retired couples strolled by. Two men jogging stood out among the holiday makers for their big rugby-type builds. He noticed them with interest. Out of habit, looking on the ground, all of a sudden James spotted a USB stick. Expecting someone to claim it on the spot, he lingered at the spot. But the village street looked sleepy, worn out by the sun.

His first thought was that *this might be important*. Not having a dad around forced him to swift decision making. Not able to stand the suspense, he decided to swing by the local library on the way home.

The volunteer at the library, must be a summer student, proved to be helpful, informing James that he had to be registered or have a library card. But after explaining the situation, the friendly student led him to an unoccupied computer.

"All yours. Let me know how you get on."

"Thanks, I appreciate the help!" He was off to a good start.

The USB stick didn't open as it normally would. James was puzzled, but unable to do anything. He pulled it out of the computer, aiming for the door.

"Any luck with it?"

"No, couldn't open it at all," James admitted.

"Do you mind if I have a go?" offered the student. Reading the surprise on James's face, he added. "I'm a bit of a dabster when it comes to technology. I haven't even been down to the beach this summer!"

James could not imagine that. However he was happy to grab this chance.

"Sure." They walked back to a computer. The student inserted the USB stick and for a few moments his hands were flying over the keys.

"This is encrypted. Positive."

"Really? What does that mean?" James shrugged his shoulders.

"You need to have a special program, like True Crypt for example, installed on a computer to access it."

"Wow. Interesting." The lad handed the USB stick back to James. After thanking him, James was deeply lost in his thoughts: *What should I to do with it now?*

3

James could not work out the psychology, how, at school time, he could barely pull himself out of bed, but on holidays he jumped out the minute he opened his eyes! Amused, he moved onto his next dilemma of the day: what to do with the USB stick?

"Mum, I think I'll swing by the library again, see if that volunteer is in again today. He will have more success with it. If I don't see him, I'll have to drop it off at the village police station." James formed his plan of action.

"Okey dokey," Leila sang back.

James could tell this place was doing wonders for his mother. He had not seen her stressed once since they arrived. A miracle indeed!

"But do be careful," she quickly added. Here we go, That was more like her. Oh well, James knew something never change.

"Bye. I will." The front door slammed behind him, shaking the cottage slightly.

The sun was burning with fierce intensity already. No wonder people with money wished to invest in property around here. The library building looked quaint: built in soft grey stone, partly covered by ivy, it resembled a bank. The green foliage around offered plenty of shade. Running up the flight of stairs, James walked the library.

The librarian, a.k.a. computer whiz, was nowhere to be seen. Maybe it was a bit early for him to start. Disappointed, James headed out. Unexpected, he spotted a face he knew he had seen before. But where? Outside, a man in his mid-twenties was putting up leaflets on the board, appealing for a lost USB stick. Unbelievable! At first, James was taken aback by such coincidence. Unbelievable! Then, still a bit hesitantly he approached the man..

"Excuse me. I found what you're looking for." James had to figure out how he knew the man first.

"You always save extra work for people? How'd you find it?" Grinning, the man was obviously very pleased.

"I was passing through the village on my way home. Were you jogging here yesterday?" James fired his own question.

"That's right. I went on a run with it in, hoping to send it off with a courier. As it turned out, it took longer than I planned for. Do you have it on you, please?"

"How do I know it's yours?" James didn't wish to appear totally gullible.

"It is encrypted. You won't be able to read it even if you tried. The information on it is of extreme importance." The answer sounded convincing enough.

"Here you go." James's suspicion was quenched.

And then the stranger added: "I'm Greg by the way and now in your debt. You must meet my friend, David as well. Then, both of us can decide how to thank you. Could you make it to the beach at noon?"

"Sure. I'll be there."

They shook hands. James felt ecstatic - what a turn of events after all!

Back at the cottage, Leila patiently listened as James's excitement poured out over his encounter with Greg.

"Darling, you must be careful. You don't know these people at all," she pleaded with him.

"Mum, there is nothing to fear. I'm meeting them in broad daylight. I'll keep my phone on."

"All right." Convinced, she finally gave in. After lunch, James grabbed the paddle board, heading towards the beach.

It was too tempting not to stop off at the only bakery in the village to get some Belgian buns. They cost an arm and a leg, but he didn't back off.

Two young men, that James would easily recognize even in a crowd, were sitting at the top of the cliffs, a perfect vista point. The Bournemouth coastline shimmered below, a deep green in colour, gradually changing into a deep turquoise, stretching for miles. James noted about eighty steps that led down to the beach, what a perfect warm up before jumping into the refreshing sea.

"Hi there!" James send off his greeting, overjoyed that Greg kept his word.

"Hi James! Meet my friend, David."

"I've heard a lot about you already," David stretched his hand to James. "You did us a huge favour, mate!"

"That's all right. I just happened to be at the right place at the right time!" James modestly pointed out.

"What do you have there?" Greg craned his neck.

"Have you been to the village bakery yet?" Feeling a bit insecure about his bold move, James shot back with the question.

"Of course, it's a favourite!" Greg sounded as though the village was packed with choice.

"That's why we run every morning, didn't you know? To justify our indulgence!" Greg patted James on the shoulder, grinning.

It was obvious he was being teased. James suspected that they weren't fitness freaks just for the sake of it. Something about these two screamed that they were on some sort of mission: super focused, organized, not leaving anything to chance. He would love to spend more time with them. Who wouldn't? He wondered what were the secrets of the USB stick, but didn't want to pry.

"I got us one each."

"We are in debt to you already as it is. It is our turn to reward you. How about tea at the Plantation Pub?"

"Ok. Cool."

"We're heading towards the King's Athletic Centre shortly. Care to join us? If you manage to finish the 5k first we'll buy you dessert as well as a main."

"You're on!" James hardly did any serious running, but there was no time like the present to get into training. If this challenge led to making two good friends, he was up for it.

"Done. But let's see what you can do on your paddle board!" David got up.

"Is your mum okay with you hanging out with us?" he added.

"Oh, yeah. You know how mothers are. She's coming down to the beach soon."

"Great, I was going to suggest that we meet her for coffee."

"She loves her lattes." James knew the minute she met them, her worries would be put to rest.

"Okay, we have a plan! I will let her know." Still not having the faintest idea what these two were involved with, he hoped for a chance to find out.

Whilst walking down to the endless stairs, they chatted as good old mates. James was bursting with a million questions to ask. Meanwhile he decided to practice his patience and endurance as Andrew had mentioned.

Why did they train so hard? What were they doing in Poole? Who do they work for? Those puzzling questions bugged as flies on a hot day. "It's good to count the blessings you already have!" He remembered his mother's words. So unexpectedly he had met these super friendly men. Was it God doing?

"Mate, you must be curious! All will be revealed in good time. You're an intelligent young man; to tell you that we are just here on holiday would be foolish," Greg stated as though reading his thoughts. James was taken back that someone actually called him intelligent. He instantly felt his confidence strengthen.

They arranged to meet with his mother at Compton Acres, famous for its Japanese Gardens.

"Are you sure that your mum doesn't mind you having tea with us?" David checked.

"Absolutely, and coffee at the Gardens will be perfect," he reassured them.

"Sounds like you know your mother well." Greg was impressed.

"I wish. It's just the two of us, so I have to make an effort. If you know what I mean."

"Yes, we do," both men nodded. "It's like our training; it's hard work but it pays off," David confirmed.

"How exactly can you relate to the 'no dad part', Greg? You have an epic dad," David grilled Greg.

"I read a lot. Mostly the classics. Gadfly made me sob when I was a teenager. Such a tragic, unnecessary misunderstanding between the father the priest, and the son, turned out revolutionary. There is no hope of ever reconciling, both ideologies will properly suck you in and will keep you bound."

"*Les Miserables* is another heart wrecking tale. It took Victor Hugo eighteen years to write it, worth reading it. It's like listening to the music in minor keys, so heart wrenching, yet full of beauty. A must for tragedy lovers!"

James was utterly impressed. Speechless, in fact. How on earth could Greg find time for exercise and read such books as a teen?

Noticing his stunned expression, Greg elaborated: "I was a shy teen. Reading made up for the lack of friends."

This James also found hard to picture.

David was in for a treat listening to their conversation. Then he joined in. "Fiction is not the same as reality, is it? Hard for me to understand with my mathematical brain."

"To have empathy with the fictional characters requires depth of heart that's for sure," Greg didn't give up easily.

"Okay. I'll agree with you on that. But there is something better than fiction. Personally, I prefer to read the Bible. There is so much instruction for our own good there.

I find it fascinating that when Jesus was asked about how to pray, He insisted on addressing God as 'Our Heavenly Father.' Jesus could have said anything else, but He called God as a Father. Such an address is full of yearning for intimacy and affection, it's truly fascinating. I love unscrambling what Jesus meant."

James could see it was true. They were always trying to get to the root of what they were discussing. He liked that. It was like watching someone playing chess skilfully or watching good tennis.

The time in great company run.

"You are some paddle-boarder!" The men were generous with compliments. James basked in such attention, going shy at first, but deep down was happier than ever.

Before they knew it, deep in another discussion, they walked up to the entrance of the Garden. Leila was waiting for them.

"We're not finished on the topic."

"Far from it!"

"Hi, mum! This is Greg and David." James beamed a smile at her.

Of medium height, with a short bob of chestnut hair that was impeccably styled, Leila eagerly shook hands with them.

"Pleased to meet you."

Before settling into a chair, David pulled hers out first, extending an invitation for her to sit down. Their manners were flawless and therefore stood out.

"Thank you. How thoughtful!"

James knew his mother always enjoyed such company.

"James is amazing on his board." Greg's praise sounded genuine.

"Oh, he certainly is."

"A rather responsible teen too. Not many of them are about. At least we don't meet many in our line of work," David also added.

"Yes, I can say that," Leila agreed. "Growing up with a mother has made him independent, no question about it, but I find it hard to admit at times."

"And it's easy to take each other for granted. We work together well, not always appreciating each other's skills." Greg opened up.

"A bit of that too." Leila already loved these men, whoever they were.

"And what exactly is it that you do?" Leila could not help her curiosity any more.

"We're not free to say just yet. In good time, God willing, it shall be revealed." David reassured with a mysterious grin on his face. "There is something important that we need to finish in Sandbanks. To say thank you for returning some vital evidence, we'd love James to join us during our training. With your permission, of course. We can vouch that James will be perfectly safe with us. His favour was career saving, really."

Coffee and fresh baklava arrived promptly, prepared by a local Kurdish chef. Foreigners brought diversity and exquisite cuisine even to Dorset. James could eat at any time of the day, feeling perpetually hungry, but this was such a treat. While enjoying hot drinks and pastries that melted away in the mouth, the bond among them grew.

"I like to be organized myself," Leila approved their plans. "Perhaps this will rub off onto James."

"I'm happy for James to join you." She gave her blessing. "Now I can relax and read to my heart's content instead of making sure James is all right on the beach! Pleasure to meet you both. Time doesn't sit still when in a good company, but now I have food shopping to do." She ruffled James's unruly hair. He was turning into a real young man almost in front of her eyes.

"I'll let you know when we are on our way back," James reassured her.

"See you soon, Leila."

Both David and Greg shook her hands with her once more.

At King's Athletic Centre, the three of them were eager to train. James knew that his fitness can't be a substitute for the lack of training.

"How is everyone today? And who is the new friend here?" The coach didn't mess about, going straight to the matter.

Why was he even doing this? He could just watch them do it. But the coach was already waiting for the introductions to follow. He eyed James from top to bottom: long, muscled legs, energetic, with a lopsided grin.

"He's with us today," explained David.

"Are you a regular runner, young man?" he demanded an answer as though the boys's life depended on it.

"Only during PE lessons." James shot an honest truth at him. He hoped that his trained legs, from hours of standing on a board, would support him now, sparing him from a massive embarrassment.

"Ah, you are in for a treat then." The coach switched in his friendly mode. It was obvious that training was not a game to him.

Now James simply had to give his best shot even if it killed him.

After a proper stretching, they lined up. David whispered, "Only be your best!"

"On your marks, set, go!" The piercing to the ear whistle made their hearts beat faster.

Both David and Greg flew past him like a gust of wind. James kept charging forward his fastest, but still was left far behind. He would never be able to catch up with them now, but he kept going. It felt as though his heart was about to jump out. Out of breath, panting for air, he could not wait for the run to be over. Watching athletes run on the TV looked deceptively easy.

"How're you doing?" David was sipping on water when James finished his track.

"Like I want to die!" James could barely speak. Everyone burst out laughing, including the coach. He seemed pleased that James didn't back out. After all, perseverance was vital to an athlete.

"Yeah, just a bit more challenging than eating baklava!" Greg teased back.

Catching his breath, James knew that eventually he would appreciate this experience; maybe after he had enough water to drink! There was a sense of comradeship and understanding among the sportsmen. The feeling that you belong somewhere, even if it included a bit of physical discomfort, was invaluable.

"Moor Valley Bike Trail tomorrow? You'll enjoy that even more. If your muscles are not in too much pain after today, of course!"

"What a question!" He could not remember ever feeling this willing to have a go at something; if only he had this motivation in school, his mum would be thrilled.

Later, at Plantation Pub, savouring delicious BBQ ribs, he was truly grateful. Even on holiday his mum could not afford for them to eat at such places. He would not mind their jobs for sure! Whatever they did for a living.

*T*he next morning, the mintute James swung his legs out of bed, the pain in his muscles shot through, as a reminder of yesterday. It felt good to be fit and able, just like his new friends. Now he was mentally prepared, realizing that without the cost of pain and sweat, nothing would improve. He welcomed a challenge and a proper breakfast was in order for him to last through the day. He might even start taking all those vitamins his mother was yammering about.

Leila offered him a banana shake with waffles. He accepted with appreciation. She raised her eyebrows, knowing better than to say anything.

"Where are you off to today?"

"First to the beach. This afternoon to the Moor Valley. We'll be biking in the forest."

"Sounds like fun! Any idea who the lads work for?"

"Not a clue, but I'm working on it." James was convinced something would slip. They lost a USB stick after all. James trusted his gut feeling.

"Perhaps they're bodyguards to a rich businessman around here. Who's a detective now?" Leila gave her best shot at guessing.

"You could be right. Will try that and see how they react."

"Or maybe they are working for a high-flying politician on holiday here?" There was no stopping Leila now. "All those detective stories that I read….hmmm…. interesting."

"Mum, do you think they trust me?" James studied her facial expression.

"Clearly, but I don't think it's their decision to make." Leila reassured him.

"I gotta run. Make sure you get some sun today too. You can't be reading indoors all the time." He could tell that they were getting along better, united by suspense.

"I will." Leila replied pleased by his sudden care.

James walked over the yellow, spongy moss towards the back gate, carefully making his way through wildly growing plants that took over the alleyway. This was the newly discovered short cut to the beach. The lush, tropical plants of Dorset thrived here. The last week of July was scorching with the temperature rising to 25 degrees by ten a.m. *How can this be endured without jumping into the sea?*

In a flash of light he was on his paddleboard. The water was clear blue nearer to the beach. James spotted jellyfish close by. He would never get tired of the sea, fresh air, and sun combined. Once he was a proper grown up, he would live in a place like this.

The lads were running late which wasn't like them. *What's holding them up?* Finally, after paddling solid for a good thirty minutes, he spotted David waving at him. James eagerly waved back. He loved spending time in their company. A few minutes later, both in wet suits, the men swam towards him. Observing them with interest, James was glad that he was a much better swimmer than runner.

"Hi there. What held you up?"

"Something unexpected came up." Greg was succinct.

"Can I be of help?" James offered eagerly.

"You know what? We might just take you up on the offer!" The answer took James by complete surprise; he almost lost balance on his board. James could tell that Greg's mind was already working out the solution. James very much hoped to be a part of it.

David, who was in front of them, gave a sign to swim back. James saw big letters on his swim hat: JESUS. *Wow! It took backbone to go out like that in public*! James filed the thought for later, hoping to ask him about it.

Eager to prove that he could be an asset, James pushed his paddle aside, challenging to race swim back. He started off with the dolphin kick, underwater to maximize his speed, leaving both of them behind. Swimming for his life, he quickly switched to the breaststroke. He only beat them both by a matter of seconds, but none the less, he did.

"Impressive," David shook the water off. "You're marine material. I hope you have enough steam to return for your board!"

"Good effort!" Greg admitted, peeling off his wetsuit.

Seeing how genuine the praise was, James knew they didn't just let him win. His own effort did it. He would happily swim back and forth to get such compliments.

"Don't overdo it as we have the bike ride later on," David reminded. He was the sensible, level-headed one among them.

"Nothing that a good lunch can't fix, hey? What about fish and chips since we are working hard?" James hoped sportsmen still ate greasy food from time to time.

"I know just the place. They fry the best fish, fresh from the sea. Lads, follow me," David ordered.

They did not need to be asked twice. Changed and packed promptly, anticipating mouth-watering food, they walked up the cliffs.

The fish and chip place looked like any other, but you could tell this was popular, as the queue stretched out of the door.

David went to place an order, while the other two grabbed a table, wood carved out of a pine tree rather skilfully, the tree stumps as chairs.

Packed in neat boxes, the fish was diffusing an appetizing aroma.

"That was quick." James was astonished.

"They really know how to do business here. Very efficient and polite, besides the amazing quality of the food. The rest of the country could learn!"

"Shall we bless the food?" Hungry, Greg was devouring the fish with his eyes.

James thought what a radical thing to do in public!

"God, thank you for providing. Bless our day and keep us safe. In Jesus' name, Amen." David's prayer was to the point.

Eating away, James knew why there was a mile long queue: crispy fish on the outside and breaking up into flakes on the inside; cooked to perfection! The chips were just right, with the right balance of salt and vinegar. "This must be by far, the best fish and chips."

Wiping his greasy hands on the paper, once more he thanked the men for lunch. Seeing that both of them had nearly finished, he seized his chance.

"Why did you put JESUS on your swim hat?"

"I thought you would never ask! That's a subject we can discuss any time!" Greg clearly enjoyed the challenge.

"Good on you for asking. Both of us believe in God."

"My mum is a believer too," James quickly pointed. "I pray to God also, but only in emergencies. A bit selfish, I know."

"Okay. Let me explain," Greg was keen.

"Even though we train hard and we look after our bodies to perform to the best of our ability, we realize that we need protection from God. Whoever says that weak people need God as a crutch hasn't really thought it through, don't you think? We are all weak and fragile in many ways. Even the strongest among us need God's help. And we are all mortal. Then what? The Bible is clear that we are created for eternity. The grave is not our final destination. God wants all people to worship Him and enjoy His love forever.

But all of us are complete sinners, so this can't happen, unless..."

"....Jesus helps us." James finished the sentence.

"Absolutely right. Spot on."

Seeing James's undivided attention, Greg carried on. "That's why Jesus, being God in the flesh, came down and died on the cross, so He can help us! Once you realize such truth, you can hardly shut up about it. One more thing, not only God want to be our Saviour, He must be our Lord and master of our lives. That's a true challenge."

Silence fell for a bit. They sat quietly for a minute or so. Then David prompted further: "Have you ever thought about a commitment like that before? Serious stuff, right?"

Overwhelmed, James wasn't sure how to answer. It was one thing that his mum went to church, yet another that David and Greg also believed the same truth.

"We are taking a trip to Newquay of Cornwall to visit the surfer's church I've heard about from a friend," Greg explained. "You are invited."

"Okay." James was more than a little curious.

"Then it is agreed. Good effort." David sounded thrilled about it.

"The Moor Valley is waiting, lads! Shall we get a move on?"

Walking to the car, James knew that there was nothing coincidental about his summer holiday.

The forest was serene, so peaceful, probably the best place to be in today's heat. The trouble was no one could prepare in advance for the heat wave. Once people got used to it a little bit, it was raining again. No wonder most conversations were centred on weather here. James loved being outdoors, surrounded by the shade of the trees. If only his lessons were outside!

They rented the bikes and set off. The lads were leading, James following them. A few other people had the same idea; the place was heaving with bikers or walkers. Speeding up the bumps and rolling down was so much fun. Finally, sweaty and tired, they made a water stop.

"How're you doing?" David was checking on James.

"All right. A bit tired now. You guys must be in the army! Who else could keep up with so much exercise, correct?" James pursued the guessing game.

Both of them enjoyed seeing how the suspense had gotten the better of him.

"No, we are not in the military, Detective James."

He was determined to keep looking for clues. It bound to happen.

When later on David and Greg were dropping James off at home, the neighbour was out. James had noticed the girl next door by the swimming pool from his window upon arrival. At the time he thought that he would never have the courage to speak with her. And here she was. Medium in height, with a long, dark brown mane of hair, she stood on her drive, chatting to a friend as it looked like.

"Do you know who she is?" David pried.

"Not yet, but I will," James was taken back by the strong sense of his own determination. *Where did that come from?*

"Good on you." Greg approved.

"See you tomorrow." They waved as he was heading towards the cottage.

As their sports car was pulling away, the girl and her friend looked curiously at James. He waved at them.

"Hi, there!"

"Hi, what's your name?"

"I'm James. And you are?"

"Ruby and this is my friend, Daisy. Nice to meet you."

"Sure."

Suddenly feeling outnumbered he began to walk towards his cottage.

"Hey! We're having a pool party tomorrow night. You'd be very welcome." Ruby extended an invite.

James felt the colour flood his face. This was his chance to brave it up.

"I'd love to come. Thanks."

5

"Good morning, son. You would not want to miss the pool party." Leila could not help but tease him.

"Good morning, mum. I'm awake." James let her know through the door.

"Did you sleep well?"

"Yes." James was not ready to discuss his true feelings.

"Good. Let's have breakfast."

In truth, the second James opened his eyes, the last reminder of yesterday dampened his spirit. Familiar restlessness grew inside him. One minute he was so eager about meeting Ruby; the next, he was panicking. He felt awkward around girls. *What should I say? Who else will be there?* Worry never was helpful when he was out of his comfort zone. *Maybe I could bring Greg and David along. Not a chance!* He had to rule out such an idea. *Didn't I read somewhere that worrying and fear were paralysing parasites? I will have to look it up again.*

James appreciated that his mother had given him more space, waiting for him to come out with his burdens on his own pace.

Scrambled eggs on toast with Innocent juice hit the spot. Feeling energized, James kissed his mother and rushed towards the beach once more. He could get used to it.

Deciding that it was silly to agonise over the pool party, he felt better for it. He would approach it in the same way as when he first learned how to dive and straight away jumped off the local pier. He will never forget the sense of being set free from his fear by facing it head on. Speeding down the cliff path, he spotted David and Greg, deep in conversation.

"Being willing is a great bonus…" He got just the tail of their conversation.

"Hi, there!" David grinned at him.

"Hiya," James shot back. "Early today. Something the matter?"

"In fact, there is." By the tone of his voice, James already knew they had decided on something. "We can use your help at last. If you're up for it."

"I was ready yesterday!" Exclaimed James.

"We're not in the military, nor protecting a politician. Good guesswork, please pass on to your mother. We're working for DASCU which stands for Drugs and Serious Crime Unit. We also partner with the international fraud department. They have brilliant computer experts there, by the way they were expecting that USB from us. Our attention is on a notorious drug dealer and his suspicious activity in Spain. We have been hunting this criminal down for some time. But after our surveillance in Dorset, we've got him. A few details left to apprehend him, preferably without much disturbance for the locals."

"Whoa! I would love to help." The excitement rushed through his veins. He was hoping this summer holiday would be different, but surely the events that were unfolding in front of him, only happened in films!

"Do you realize, this can be dangerous? I must warn you," as a matter of fact stated David. He was always willing to take a necessary risk, but cautious and clearheaded.

"It'll be just like in films; the bad guys always lose." James gave a smug answer.

"Nothing in real life is like in films, I'm afraid. Plenty of good guys get injured and killed, for the cause of good. That's why we always train hard, but also pray. We can use you in 'Operation Pizza'. We had to ask you first if you're willing, but now, since you are, we need to get you clearance from our superiors."

James and the lads shook hands. "Let's go for a swim. Then we'll have BBM go over details. Sound good?"

"What does BBM stand for?" James had to know.

"Basic Briefing Meet," Greg explained.

"Sounds perfect." James was thrilled being part of what they did. He could not fish for a better company this summer or ever. There was little doubt that his one desperate, selfish prayer was being answered that soon. The sheer mystery of God, whose love was unconditional, blew his mind off.

After prolonged swim, tired and happy, they landed in the village cafe. Buns were ordered along with two coffees and one hot chocolate. David explained that they learned about this drug dealer from Spanish police. Since he moved his dealing back to UK, they had been keeping their eyes on him. He was the owner of a villa in Sandbanks with a legitimate business selling chemicals for swimming pools, a perfect money laundering cover. But this hadn't fooled them. He was kept on a short leash and didn't even know it.

"Nothing can replace old fashioned police work. We were checking his every move!" David was pleased.

"Life is good in tropical Dorset, with its sun and sea, glorious views. And the best fish and chips are such a bonus. Who could blame him for choosing this paradise to settle in, just as good as Marbella. Except this time, the enjoyment will be cut short." Concluded Greg.

"What we're hoping to do, is to send you in, looking unsuspicious. In fact, a large pizza order has been placed from the house for Friday. One of the body guards is our recruit. He is waiting for the signal from us that everything is in place and we are ready to act. It's too risky to use the phone to contact him. You can be our eyes and ears. Pay attention to the details, it might be useful. Your script for your contact goes like this:

You will say, "Are you surfing much?

The recruited body guard will respond, "Yes, but my board needs waxing."

You reply, "What technique are you using?"

His reply, "I prefer lines."

"Here lies the clue: if he says circles, there is a problem. But if it is lines, that is a signal for us to move in."

"Sounds good, sir!" James still could hardly believe that this was for real.

"Don't get your hopes up yet! They don't always approve of using civilian help, plus you are still such youth, no offence here. But we need to work as low key as possible in such a prestigious area. The less noise we make about it, the more praise we get." David considered the tiniest of details. Now everything made sense. Their actions were always super organized and thought out. *An international fraud*

department, huh? Met officers from a special division! James smiled.
Who would have guessed?

"How did you come across this drug dealer initially?"
James had more questions than before. "I'd love to hear all
the details."

David and Greg looked at each other. Greg gave a
nod.

"We hope you'll be of help. You have a right to know
the details."

James nodded to confirm.

"One thing we have learned is that no matter how
deceitfully ingenious the plan, it can fail with one mistake.
However, when I lost the USB stick that contained all the
intelligence about his money dealing on the net, you were an
answer to prayer - God was covering for me. Prayer works."

"The local police in Marbella got a report about a
rather strange business activity. A business, advertising water
cooling systems, popped up in the area. The lorries moved
throughout the day and night. Spaniards are tight and tough.
They would always save money instead of spending it on
comfort any day. They had enjoyed their siesta for centuries,

during the heat of the day. What Spanish restaurant would need a cooling system for?" The men chuckled. " Such busy activities, while no one was investing in the cooling systems, raised questions. Nothing escapes the eyes of the locals. When police looked into a report from one of them, the documents for the business were in order and the storage units empty. But the police trusted their instincts, not putting the matter to rest just yet. They got the sniffer dogs on site. Traces of drugs were found. The company shut down and so called 'Mr. Espinoza' vanished."

"We were charged with tracking him down, dead or alive! Not an easy task, but with hard work and patience, he popped up in Poole under the name Mr. Bugsworth, this time with a legitimate business selling chemicals for pools. No trace of drugs. Finally our computer experts traced drug money hidden in bitcoins. He can't escape this time. What the Spanish police began, we will finish. Does this satisfy your well endured curiosity young man?"

"Hold on. What are bitcoins?"

"Bitcoins are digital currency. They're created and held electronically. No banks are involved, making it hard to trace."

"Cool. Will I have some kind of weapon?" James's imagination had no stopping now.

"You are an ordinary delivery boy. Not a super spy! If our superiors approve you, I'm sure we can find you a gadget to use. Let's not get ahead."

"Yes, sir!" James was already on the mission. "And I was nervous about the party…"

"What party? Did that good mannered girl next door give you an invitation?" David was back to his normal, relaxed self, the wrinkles between his eyes gone.

"Nothing escapes you, does it?" Now James knew they were highly trained professionals. He just grinned back.

"Her name is Ruby," An affection rang in his voice. James hadn't met a girl like her before. She was so daring, sporty and sweet all at the same time.

"Any tips needed?" Greg displayed his concern.

"Oh, I'll be fine. Do either of you have a girlfriend?"

"No time for luxuries," David was blunt. "Criminals are running on the loose, you know."

Noticing how serious James took it, he continued. "Not really. God is still working on my masterpiece. I'm not worried. God's timing and plan are perfect," Greg explained.

"You will be fine. We will pray for you. Good manners are the answer with ladies. Works every time," Greg worked out his theory on women.

"Thanks guys, for everything. I better go." James's mind was racing elsewhere.

"Okay, one last thing, you understand this is top secret? The only person you can mention this to is your mother. We must have her permission."

"Not a chance! My mother will never agree to this!"

"I'll chat with her about it when I drop you off." David was adamant.

"This will not be cool by her. Only a miracle will make her say yes." James knew well.

"Let God work on her heart, shall we?"

David prayed for God to prepare her heart.

On the way home, David stopped off at the supermarket. He got two gorgeous bouquets of roses; one for Leila, and one for Ruby. He explained, "Consider the job done, mate. Just have to smile and use your charm, the rest is easy because God has already paved the way!" James envied his confidence.

Leila kept staring at the gorgeous bouquet in front of her. Then she didn't trust her ears.

"What? James spying on a dangerous drug dealer? This is an insane idea!" David could not say he had not been warned!

"Mrs. Orwell, we must deal with this criminal activity fast and sure, which unfortunately is spreading like cancer. James has helped us already. The trouble is, these evil people involve kids younger than James to distribute drugs. Cheap labour, you see. We must strike at the head; one prosperous drug dealer at a time. They would not hesitate twice about grooming a nine-year-old for the job. Ponder that. Many innocent kids' lives are at stake. We can all do our bit. I'm no Churchill, but just like during the war when the strength of the enemy was overwhelming, we found more strength. We stood for what was right and just. Simple as that." David presented the matter.

His argument almost convinced her. Almost, but not quite. Noticing her son looking taller all of a sudden, then gazing at the stunning flowers, she had to decide.

"Still this is the most ridiculous idea. But strangely enough, I have peace about it."

"Oh, good," David approved her reaction. "We have tremendous resources at our disposal this time. Wouldn't you love to see the headlines of the papers: 'Teen helps bring a super dangerous drug dealer down.'"

"Sounds terrific to me." James butted in.

"One criminal at a time." Leila echoed David's words.

"Sometimes it takes only one courageous man to start the downfall of evil. Wilberforce, for example. He wasn't willing to take the nonsense of slavery in spite of so many endorsing it," contributed Greg with much passion in his voice.

Somehow, they were all in sync now. Greg's mobile rang, breaking up the perfect harmony of the moment.

"Yes. Of course. Yes. Most definitely, Sir!" Greg had a big grin, not able to hide his feelings.

"James is approved."

"Here I come, Agent Orwell... and, of course, let's hope there will be no real danger," James added promptly.

"James Matthew, this is not a spy game! You do not understand how evil these people are," Leila wasn't easily fooled.

"All right, Mother. I will be super careful."

"We won't be far, but keep the distance to avoid suspicion. Other agents will also be nearby, ready to act!"

"We'll fight them also on our knees. In our prayer closets. And in our prayer meetings," she added with much conviction in her voice. "This is an invisible, of spiritual dimension war, but none the less a war!"

"Mum, God will watch our back! Can I be excused please? Need to get ready for tonight. " In his head he was at the party since yesterday.

"Sure. Take care, I will see you later," Leila sent him an air kiss.

"Behave yourself, an agent!"

6

A great deal of time was wasted in front of the mirror. James had to do something about his out of control, curly and now bleached by the sun, light brown hair. First impressions are important, he agreed with whoever first said that. The end result was satisfactory, in spite of the fact that all the natural hair products his mother forced on him weren't the popular brand. But hey, he was getting used to unusual things happening! "Why use chemicals unnecessarily? They kill the sea life you love so much!" Leila would point out. This actually made sense. What typical teenager thinks of that unless he was a geek? All the weird things his mum applied to herself: rose hip oil and olive leaves weren't his peers' choice. Surprisingly, what his friends influence seemed to fade.

"You must learn not to follow the crowd. Be a leader!" James heard her, but in practice this was a real challenge.

The walk next door took less than five minutes, hardly long enough to calm the nerves down. He mused upon David and Greg's banter over his shyness: "Oh, yes, he's got this one." Reflecting on that made him randomly smile.

Ruby opened the door straight away as though she had been lingering nearby. In her polka dot dress with her silky hair tight at the back and a touch of lip gloss she looked older. Loud music blasting in the background silenced as he stared at her joyful, sincere face.

"Hi, I'm glad you made it." Ruby stretched her hand to him.

"Thanks for the invite." James swallowed hard, stepping inside.

The garden was larger than at the cottage where they were staying. There was an enormous patio with tables and chairs. The flowers were difficult to spot in the dark, but a balmy breeze was effectively diffusing the aroma of roses. A keen gardener, which he suspected was one of her parents, invested some time here. Lanterns and outdoor lights were hanging high in the air. The lit fire in the Chiminea attracted night insects.

Both of them landed near the fire with a glass of cold lemonade each.

"Where are you from?" Ruby boldly made a first move.

"I'm from a small village called Shepherd's Well which is in Suffolk. It's near Bury St. Edmunds, a historic town nearby. Have you ever been?"

"No. I've always lived in Dorset, Sandbanks, so the sea is always within walking distance; I can't imagine if it wasn't."

"You are so fortunate!" James could not help express his envy. It was so easy to talk to Ruby as though he had known her for a long time. He liked to name people with letters, an annoying habit to be sure. She was already a triple PPP in his mind: pure, pleasant, perfect. Meeting her was not a coincidence. James sensed that there was a change in him.

He realized that there was a purpose and meaning to everything that happened in life. Even this little holiday was a good illustration of that: how they stopped off in Brighton; the conversation with Andrew still burned on his mind; meeting David and Greg who were believers and had an important task of stopping evil; and now Ruby. All these wonderful people, suddenly, all at once turned up in his life just like that, but it was worth the wait. Maybe God planned it all along, who knew?

Ruby noticed that James was somewhere else.

"Penny for your thoughts?" She had a heart-melting smile.

"I was just thinking how I've met the most amazing people on this holiday already and it's not even over yet!"

"Really, who else did you meet?" Ruby genuinely was interested.

"Oh, mostly guys, you are the only girl so far, besides your friend Daisy, of course," he added with haste.

"I can live with that," Ruby commented happily.

James beamed from ear to ear. She was such a pleasant person to be around, easy to talk to and, most important to him was that he could be himself, just like when he was out in the sea.

"Do you like swimming?" He realized this was a silly question, asking anyway.

"Yes, I go most days in the summer. Can't bare the cold, so have to make the most of it. Fortunately there are always plenty of sunny days in Sandbanks."

"Tell me about it. I'm so envious! Shall we go tomorrow together? I have a paddleboard with me," James added.

"Yeah, why not? I would love to. A few of my closest friends are on holiday abroad at the moment. It's an outrage to go elsewhere while the weather is so great here."

"I completely agree. We went to Andalucia in October last year. It was the best time and no tourists."

Ruby seemed mature for her age. What just happened? James was amazed how easy it was to talk to a girl after all. Her warm, assured, calm personality, sweeping mane of chestnut hair and dancing from inner joy eyes fascinated him. As they sat by the fire, the warm glow embraced James's face and a deep contentment flooding in.

The time to say goodbye came too quickly. This was the most enchanted evening of his life. But there was a new day to look forward to on the beach tomorrow... with Ruby... music to his ears. He only had to find a way to explain this to the lads! Oh, the shock on their faces at how fast things were progressing.

James's mind suddenly began to race. Should he give her a peck on the cheek or shake hands? Maybe just a warm smile like Greg would do. He hardly knew this girl and there was certainly no harm in showing respect.

"Bye, I've enjoyed this evening very much," James smiled as wide as he could, shaking Ruby's hand with energy.

"Ouch, you have an iron grip!"

"So sorry. This must be of holding an oar." This was definitely a new learning curve. Maybe this was not as straightforward as diving after all?

"See you tomorrow then," he waved from the drive.

"See ya!" Ruby waved and returned his smile. Dragon flies were zooming unaware that something timeless was born tonight here: it was stronger than the aroma of the flowers, more powerful than the ocean waves, more blinding than a bright sun. James walked towards the cottage, intoxicated by his first crush. This overpowering feeling that caused him to think about another human being all the time, was completely new to him. Suddenly he also had to know: "Was this how God felt about him? Did He always love him even when James couldn't care less about Him?" The questions started to pile up, demanding all the answers. He would get to the bottom of it, maybe once he started reading the Bible!

The mobile beeped. A text from David read: "Hope the evening went well. Thinking of you. Speak soon, D."

James replied right away.

"Never had a better time. Thank you. Ruby is joining us at the beach. See you in the morning! J."

Leila was still up, reading in bed.

"All right, darling?"

"Yes, I had the best time." He sat on the edge of her bed and they chatted about his time next door, James letting her in on all the details. Leila could not believe how happy her son lately. She welcomed such a transformation. What a holiday it turned out to be.

"I'm so happy for you… pleased that you are enjoying yourself and having such a good time. Your new friends are amazing! I can't wait to meet Ruby too," she added with a wink.

"Good night, mum!"

"Good night, son. Rest well."

As James was walking up the stairs to his room, he suddenly realized the strength and confidence that he hadn't thought possible had come, shaping him into a completely different person. Most importantly, the bond and appreciation between him and his mum, almost absent a few weeks ago, started to form between them.

oday James was going to the beach with Ruby! The thought washed over him warmly. Feeling content in his heart, James scrubbed himself fiercely, tapping into his mother's wild rose balm for his hair. Getting ready in no time, James was ringing Ruby's door bell.

A tall man with the dimples, introduced to him as Ruby's father last night, opened the door. James could see the likeness of him in Ruby. The same determination and assurance was strikingly obvious.

"Ah, James, good to see you again," he extended a cheerful welcome.

"Please, come through. Come on in. Ruby's not quite ready. Women!" He looked hilarious while energetically rolling his brown eyes to back up his point.

There was no mockery in his words, it rather hinted that his mind was occupied elsewhere. James, on the other hand, didn't mind being in his fascinating daughter's world, even if it involved a bit of waiting now and then.

"Hi James," shouted Ruby from upstairs. "I'll only be a moment."

"No rush. The beach isn't moving anywhere." Did he just say that?

"Did you have breakfast?" Ruby popped her head over the bannister, wondering.

"Not yet." James suddenly remembered that he failed his new resolution, rushing out. His recent behaviour baffled even him. He would have to think about it later.

"Go through to the kitchen, on your left, my mother made some fresh smoothie. She is a pro when it comes to health drinks. You'll see."

"Thanks."

James followed her clear instructions. The blender was full of goodness, so he helped himself to it. Looking out of the French doors into the garden, he saw her mother was fussing over the plants. She must have sensed his stare; looking up, she energetically waved to him. James was convinced this must be the friendliest family. He hardly knew them, yet felt so comfortable being around. Surely, not all people in Poole were like them!

"Good morning." He greeted Ruby's mother warmly, stepping on to the patio.

"Morning! I've heard all about you. Last night I was out, so we weren't properly introduced. I'm Venetia."

"I'm James. Pleased to make your acquaintance."

"Wow, you know how to make a lasting impression on a lady!"

"My mother doesn't give up hope. I must be the most shy and stubborn teenager there is, but now seeing the effect of her training, I'll always follow her advice. I hope you will meet her soon."

"Oh, this sounds serious."

James turned the colour of her most wonderfully blooming roses, deep red.

"Never mind. I do like to tease. Enjoy your time on the beach." She carried on with her gardening.

"Thank you." James was only too happy to make his escape, forgetting to compliment her on her smoothie or garden. She was friendly, but not as easy as her daughter or husband to chat with. It was obvious that Venetia thrived to have everything under control.

Ruby appeared just at the right moment wearing a flowery dress, her silky hair pulled up in a fancy bun, with one strand along her high cheek-boned face. James hadn't mixed with girls much before meeting Ruby. Just looking at her made him feel a bit awkward. *Why on earth does she want to hang out with me?*

"I see you found the smoothie. And my mother. She is alright, but can be rather intimidating at first. You'll get used to it. I prank her occasionally. Do you want to hear something funny?" Not waiting for a reply, she chatted away as they walked out.

"One time I was going to prank my dad, but my mum fell for it. I wished I'd filmed it."

"What happened was, mum came home from work late, she's a party planner by the way, parched for a cuppa…." As Ruby's voice was lulling him into her simple and wonderful world, James thought that how even a day before, he lived his life, not suspecting a thing and now he could not imagine a day without Ruby in it. How could this even be possible? He just foolishly smiled back, while walking with her towards the beach and basking in such simple happiness of life.

Enjoying James's attention, Ruby carried on: "She unsuspectedly picked up a cup, which was upside down; I had to practice with the help of YouTube to master it, and took it off the shelf. Floods of water gushed out from underneath it." James chuckled.

"Then, still not with it, she pulled another cup and again, the water spilled out," Ruby clearly enjoyed retelling the story.

James was almost in hysterics.

"Determined, she pulled the third cup out. I still can't believe that she chose the exact cups that I set up in a row. The water was all over the kitchen floor. At that point she didn't care for the cup of tea anymore."

Both Ruby and James were laughing their heads off by now.

"Did, she… get.. her …cup ..of …tea in the end?" James squeezed the question out.

"Yes! I mopped the floor and made her a cuppa!"

"You are a dark horse, Ruby! I have been warned. Thanks for the heads up."

Ruby, feeling like a proper prankster, savoured the effect of her story.

David and Greg were already sitting in one of the cafés on the beach, sipping their morning coffee. They looked relaxed. James spotted them fast enough, knowing now that their tourist look was a sheer cover up. Even so, his mates were the most focused, on guard, extremely vigilant men he had ever met. *How do they do it?* He could never understand how they could blend in so well with the rest of the tourists. Once, David indulged his curiosity, explaining: "Because we need some rest just like anyone else. Our training is always present, but it is like a wet suit, when you take it off, but your swimming abilities are still with you." This was not as simple as that to James. He hoped he could pretend just as well during Operation Pizza. He must not try too hard, but be himself. He was glad that both David and Greg didn't expect him to be anything, but a willing help. This he could do.

"Hi guys. This is Ruby," he said as casually as possible whilst introducing her. He hoped that they would approve of her, which meant everything to him.

"Delighted to meet you – we've heard a lot about you." Greg was charm itself. And Ruby suddenly feeling shy.

James knew that they would not make it totally easy for him, but they cared and looked after him well. He could trust that they would not embarrass him. James could live with teasing here and there.

"And I've heard of both of you!" Ruby volleyed back, barely suppressing her nervous giggles. Her relaxed, down-to-earth personality shined through.

James's happiness, like a strong dose of sunshine, was impossible to hide.

The men exchanged a meaningful look. This did not escape James's observation. *What will they decide to do?* The situation was taking an unexpected turn by adding Ruby to the equation. Submitting to their decision was not negotiable, he knew that much.

"Ruby, we have planned to have a BBM today to go over some crucial details with James today. He is helping us with something important. We trust you. Can we count on you being confidential about it?" David almost pulled out the right answer from those he addressed, not leaving a choice.

"Sure thing. What does BBM stand for?" Ruby inquired politely, but dying to know.

"Basic Briefing Meet." David explained good-naturedly.

James was appreciative that they were discerning not only about the crooks and criminals, but good people like Ruby. Words could not describe his relief at this point. It would be a challenge to hide his involvement from Ruby.

Ruby gave him a nudge, as though wondering, *what's this all about?* If she only knew! He sent her a just-wait-till you-hear-it look back. What a pair they would make; having a go at playing charades. James had read somewhere that most communication is done by body language.

"I'd love to join you, if that's ok," she replied with the element of surety.

"It's settled then. If you two swim now, you can meet us back at our place later?" David offered.

Ruby was an accomplished swimmer just as James had expected. When she told him that she loved to sing, it took him by surprise. Apparently she even tried to launch a YouTube channel with her own songs. "If I didn't struggle with self-doubt, with thoughts that I'm not good enough, that would be a problem solved," she honestly admitted. "I've tried to talk one of my school friends into singing with me, but without much success!"

"My mum is an opera singer," James mentioned casually as they swam along.

"Are you serious?" Before he knew what was happening, Ruby started wildly splashing about.

"Will she give me some lessons?" She had to ask. James could not imagine having such a dose of excitement over singing! But then he was just as passionate about paddle boarding, perhaps not outwardly, but all the same.

"I'll ask, I promise. But if you don't control your excitement, the life guards will think they have a job to do!"

"You don't understand. I was hoping for someone to coach me. This would be a dream come true. Oh, if only you lived closer. You love the sea; I love to sing; makes perfect sense." Ruby was on a mission. "A bit of excitement isn't a bad thing. I wish my father could see that. He is such a reserved Englishman at times. It's amazing we're related to each other."

The time flew by in the company that he enjoyed so much. James glanced at his second most cherished possession, a waterproof watch.

"We'd better pack up and meet the lads. Shall I drop you off at home or would you like to join us?" In spite of their invitation to include her, James wanted to make sure.

"I'd love to come. Most of my friends are away. I thought I'd be bored stiff. This summer break is looking up!"

James was flattered. It was so great to know that she seemed pleased about being a part of their plans, even though she didn't know exactly what was going on yet. They began to walk up the cliffs toward the café.

Ruby naturally slipped her hand into his before James realized how it happened. He gave her a squeeze approvingly. He was concerned that her parents wouldn't approve of their fast developing friendship. Deciding not to dwell on the unknown, he embraced the moment.

The walk to the top of the cliffs, that previously seemed so laborious, was over too soon alongside Ruby. James could have walked with her like this forever, but time was of the essence; they had a criminal to catch. James was anxious to hear the instructions from David and Greg concerning his part. He checked the address that David had texted him.

"Ruby, do you know where Pine Lane is?"

"Sure. We're not too far. Follow me." She confidently took the lead. Before he could count to ten, they were standing outside number 29 on Pine Lane.

James rang the bell. The door flung open.

"What took you so long, kids?" Greg invited them in.

"A cold drink anyone?" he offered casually.

"Yes, please," they both echoed back.

"The pair of you make a good double act." Greg grinned in David's direction, seeking a back up.

"In catching criminals . . . 'cause I don't sing!" James cleared up the matter.

"Oh, I get the point. Down to business then. Let's grab our drinks and go to the launch," David was all business now. Observing his skills, James was determined to train himself to be a leader like him. So far he was only good at following the crowd, especially while in school.

Ruby, not sure what exactly to expect yet, picked a pair of sunglasses off the table and stepped out on the balcony. "Wow, where did you get these glasses from? James, have a try!" A boat, a small dot before, suddenly was right in front of his nose.

"Good, isn't it?" Greg could not help but comment. "But play time is over."

"We're here on a drug dealer handling task. James can fill you in on all the details later. On Friday night James is going to deliver pizza in Sandbanks. He will have to make contact with the security in the house. This should not raise any suspicion. The rest of us will be on standby. Enough excitement for you?" David wondered.

Nodding, James embraced every minute being a part of an undercover operation.

"This is really happening," he muttered under his breath.

"In our most sleepy village?" It was Ruby turn to be surprised.

"Indeed, in the village." All three confirmed by a nod.

"If all goes to plan we'll have time for a trip to the Surfer's church on Sunday. James is coming. A good friend of mine, who travels down to the Board Masters competition each year, told me about it," added Greg for Ruby's sake. James could not tell what sounded more exciting to him; a trip to Newquay or the finale of the operation.

"What do you think of such a plan then? "

Ruby was sitting on the edge of her chair, ready to say something.

"I had no idea and I live here. Can I be of any help?"

"I suppose you can serve tea to James's mother to calm her nerves down," stated Greg in a rather serious voice.

"May I ask which house James is going to deliver pizza to?" She would not be shaken off easily.

"It's still classified information. We trust you, but rules are there to obey, not break!"

Both James and Ruby looked back at them with understanding.

"Ok. And I've never been to church before. Sounds interesting."

"If you don't mind we would love to pray together and commit this whole operation to the Lord. Will you pray with us, Ruby?"

"Of course. I've never prayed before, but wouldn't mind joining you." She gave her honest answer.

"Father God, thank you for watching over us. We commit James into Your hands. Please protect him during this assignment. Guide us to the best way to disarm this criminal who brings pain and destruction with his evil activity. Amen."

"I've never thought about God as a Father, a person you can be so familiar with."

"There is always so much to learn, when we are open to it, isn't it?" David pointed out.

Friday evening arrived soon enough. James was more than ready, keeping his nerves under control. The pizza delivery uniform was not flattering. Focused on the task ahead, he had to ignore such vain details. The hat was fiddly, pushing his unruly hair down, but he was too excited to care.

"The man in charge of the pizza shift has been warned if anyone wants to check your employment." Greg, showing a father's care, winked at him.

"Yes, sir. I got that!" James shouted before speeding away on the scooter. His mother and Ruby gave a final wave.

"He'll be fine. This criminal doesn't have a clue. He thinks he's invisible, as most of them do! Mistake number one!" David reassured everyone.

"Shall we go for a cuppa?" Linking arms with Leila, Ruby steered her towards the house.

Loaded with freshly baked pizza, James rehearsed the address he had been given and proceeded to the destination.

A Google map delivered nicely. He slowed to a stop as he rolled up to the massive iron gate. Pressing the buzzer, he spoke to the camera, "Pizza delivery."

The uniformed security man checked the CCTV and let him in. The gate opened slowly and he carried on scooting up the steep hill. The mansion towered at the very top. Finally, reaching the door, James rang the bell, spotting a light blue Aston Martin convertible perched by the pristine looking front lawn. He could not take his eyes off such beauty for a minute or two.

A hulky wired man in black opened the front door. After giving him a full body scan, he ushered him into the front room. "Thanks," James mumbled back, the reality of the moment dawning on him.

"I'll be a moment. Don't go anywhere." James knew that his stern voice demanded full cooperation, so he put his bag on the floor, looking around coolly. There were two more security men in the house. One black-suited security, with a non expressive face, moved towards him, collecting the pizza bag. The other one was busy listening to his earpiece.

James assumed he was about to receive a tip. But which one was his contact? He kept looking around, thinking fast. Beyond the entrance hall, stretched an Olympic size swimming pool, screaming of wealth. At the same precise moment, a boy, around six years old shouted, "Mum, see what I can do!" And off he went with the big splash.

The summer evening was still pleasant, but the heat of the day was gone. The boy's mother, showing off her shapely figure and BVLGARI sunglasses, sat by the pool flicking through a Vogue.

There was also a toddler girl, who perched contentedly by the side of the pool. Then she decided to copy her brother. Before James realized it, she was in the water, gasping for air. Everything happened in a split of a second. With no time for thinking, James tore towards the pool. "IPhone" shot through his mind. Chucking it on the floor, he jumped in. The girl was going under, kicking in panic. James had no idea how to get a good grip on her. "God, help!" Suddenly the girl went still. The mother, panicking, screamed repeatedly, "My baby! Oh, my baby girl!" James with a firm grip on her now, he pushed towards the edge of the pool. The mother paced with her arms open, ready to receive the child.

James passed the girl, then pulled himself out, dripping everywhere.

"She swallowed lots of water. We must make her spit it out!"

"Go ahead! Do you know what to do?" Her mother was still badly shaken up. James started mouth to mouth resuscitation. Soon enough, the girl was coughing up water.

James breathed a sigh of relief.

"Thank you! You are a God-send! You just got yourself the biggest tip a pizza man ever received. Wait till my husband hears about it!"

Her brother, also out of the pool, was observing everything with his eyes wide open, not saying a word.

"Would you like a drink? Please don't go anywhere. I'll take my daughter upstairs away from this dreadful pool and change her clothes." A security guard returned, puzzled at the scene.

"What just happened?" he whispered to James.

"The toddler fell into the pool."

As the mother passed them, carrying her daughter upstairs, she gave a murderous look to the security. "Utterly useless!" she spat at them angrily.

"Thank you. I can't imagine what would've happened if it weren't for you. They'll never give me a good reference for UBS now." His words were pained.

"What's that?" James wondered, drying himself off with the towel he found by the pool.

"Universal Bodyguard Service." The man's voice sounded weepy. "Where on earth did you learn to react so fast?" He openly admired his reaction.

James thought this was the right moment to pass the message. Suddenly sensing every nerve ending in his body, James asked, "Are you surfing much?"

"Yes, but my board needs waxing."

Relieved that the message was going through, James braved up.

"What technique are you using?"

"I prefer lines."

They were on! James could hardly contain himself, but carried on as naturally as he could.

To avoid any suspicion, they carried on casually chatted for a bit.

"I paddle on my board all year round pretty much. You have to be a good swimmer. Crazy stuff happens in the water. I wouldn't mind being a lifeguard to be honest."

"Oh, you most definitely could be."

"I think that chlorine burned my mouth. Can I have a drink of something, please?"

"You most certainly deserve it. Make yourself at home. Here are some more towels for you." The security pointed in the direction of the guest room.

James didn't wait long. Remembering to grab the phone, he stepped in, looking around with much interest. The walls were covered in beautiful, enlarged photos of different places around the world: Mexico, Colombia, Peru, Afghanistan, Indonesia, Bolivia. Deep in his subconscious, James knew the photos were linked by an invisible connection. When he began to dry himself, a sim card, hidden in the towels, dropped on the floor. Fast as a cat, he picked it up and carried on drying himself as best he could.

Feeling like his mission was done here, he decided to leave discreetly. The lady of the house scared him more than the security. She was certainly shaken up and probably had gone upstairs for her own sake. He picked up his delivery bag, aiming towards the front door.

The balmy breeze in the evening was pleasant, but not pleasant enough if you were wet. James barely had time to change out of his still soaking uniform before everyone circled him with their curiosity and demanding questions.

David shouted out. "Wait a minute. One person at a time. Give the lad a break!"

Silence fell. Then James described what had happened up at the house.

"I get the feeling that one security man doesn't like his boss very much, just doing the job for a bit of money.

The other one made contact after we exchanged the code, passing on this sim card to us. James carefully extracted the item.

"Good effort," praised David.

"Excellent work, James. I'll get our surveillance men to check the photos right away!" Greg was on it pronto.

As they were chatting, admiring his quick responses, the doorbell rang. David pressed his index finger to his lips, waving everyone to hide in the garden. Leila, taking her time, went to answer the door.

"Good evening, madam! Does James Orwell live here?" The man at the door inquired.

Not showing her amusement, or wishing to lie, Leila hesitated for a moment.

"Who's asking for him?"

"I'm a security guard for the family at the hilltop house, where he just delivered a pizza."

"Oh yes. I will get him for you." Leila vigorously waved to James.

James could not believe the speed he was found. Surely it had been an hour at the most. The security man must have inquired at the pizza place. Phew, what a good job the shift manager had been warned.

"Why did you rush away so quickly? I gave you my best approval. Mr. Bugsworth has a reward for you."

"Here." The man handed him an envelope.

"Thank you! Would be great to stay in touch."

"Sure. Here is my contact number." The man handed his business card out.

"Speak to you soon!" James vigorously shook his hand.

The minute the front door of the cottage got shut, everyone flew back inside.

"Let's see how generous Mr. Bugsworth is!"

James tore the paper with one hand and handed the business card to David with the other.

There was a hand-written thank you card with a cheque for one hundred pounds. "Not bad for a tip." James looked at everybody, lifting the cheque up in the air. "Some pizza delivery!"

"Well deserved, mate. Keep it as a bonus." David patted him on the back approvingly.

"That's what they would pay to a kid to deliver a shoebox full of drugs. To lure them in!" explained Greg.

"I know who Mr. Bugsworth is!" Finally it dawned on Ruby. "He sells pool chemicals at discounted prices. My dad always orders from him."

"What a small world," Greg cheered. The sense that all loose ends were coming together about this man hung in the air.

"Why didn't you mention that before, young lady?" David inquired.

"Maybe it's because his name was classified?" Ruby shot the witty answer back.

"A score for Ruby. We'll be wrapping this up ASAP," David announced. James straightened his back, making his shoulders seem broader. With a new sense of pride, feeling useful, he stood tall.

"Then tonight everyone is invited for a BBQ; our treat." A warm invite came from Leila. "My old friends will be joining us from Brighton, so you can all meet them. Ruby, please extend an invitation to your parents."

"Will do. Thank you." Ruby wanting to please Leila, looking forward to their first singing session.

"How can we help?" David offered.

"Oh, you have enough on your plate. This is my time to entertain." Leila reassured him.

James thought it would be simply epic if Ruby gave him a hand at decorating the garden. What an astonishing surprise this would be for his mother.

"I think we should give your mother a hand, don't you?" Ruby said as though reading his mind.

"Any ideas what we can do?"

"Plenty. My mother has everything in her shed. Let's go and have a look."

"Ingenious!" Doing it together was an added bonus.

"Come on, follow me." Determined, marching out in her flip flops along the path that was covered up in pine cones, Ruby led the way. James really like her sense of colour: a flowery top and plain skirt suited her. She must be really good at this sort of thing, decorating. The walk to her house took a few minutes. Soon enough they were ransacking the shed for appropriate decorations. Her mother was serious about her business. There was a ton of stuff: bunting, paper flowers, glass lanterns, outdoor lights, candle holders and much more.

"Why on earth does she need all these things?"

"Oh, you know, she has these items available for hire."

After a good sorting out, they had chosen the right deco. James was relieved that Ruby seem to know what to do. As they were walking up the driveway, loaded with cardboard boxes partly blocking the vision, a voice that James recognized, offered: "Need any help?" It was none other than Andrew walking towards them with a broad smile.

"What do you say about Dorset then? A place as good as it gets in this country if you ask me," Andrew didn't wait for the answer. The men hugged fondly.

"Hi, this is Ruby. When did you get here? Have you been by the beach yet? Did you bring the dogs with you?" James fired his questions like bullets.

"Not yet, was waiting for you. I tell you, I've had enough sitting in the car for one day, not to mention the dogs. Please, allow me," Andrew carefully transferred the boxes from Ruby into his arms.

"Thanks, it's kind of you."

"Andrew used to be in the Navy," James felt as though he didn't introduce Andrew properly. "Just wait till you see his Dalmatians!"

"Good timing too with the action about to take place!" Ruby's words just jumped out. Feeling guilty, she looked at James in anticipation, hoping he could fix her leak.

"I think if anyone could help, it would be him. He still has a dry suit from the Navy days, imagine that?"

Not sure what exactly they were on about, Andrew seemed perplexed.

"I wonder, what happened to old James I was hanging out with in Brighton?" he noticed the change.

Then he carried the boxes straight to the garden patio.

"How about the two of you go some catching up while I get on with the garden for tonight?" Ruby offered unselfishly.

"Sounds like a plan to me," Andrew agreed.

"Are you absolutely sure? I was ready to help." James didn't feel right to leave all the work for Ruby.

"I'll do what I can on my own. It wouldn't be the first time and if I need help with anything, I'll shout. Perhaps you can hang the lights for me at the end."

"It's a deal. Thanks." James didn't need to be asked twice.

Ruby found the dogs adorable. "Can James and I walk them tonight?"

"Of course! They demand three walks per day, a serious responsibility for the owner. Take them off my hands any time you wish." Andrew meant it.

James had to check with his superiors about letting Andrew in the know first. As the two of them walked down to the beach with the dogs running along, James told Andrew the events of the week, savouring details of "Operation Pizza". James was informed that Monday would be the day when the apprehension of the drug dealer would happen.

"Looks like we arrived in time for the most exciting part. I'm in if I can be of any help." Andrew seemed revived now.

"Thanks, I didn't expect anything else from you, Andrew." Once again James felt admiration for him.

The sea was clear, no wind; the blue sky was endless; the temperature was slowly losing its heat.

"We couldn't have a better day," Andrew stated happily. "It was windy in Brighton, as usual, when we left. No screeching seagulls here either. Those noisy, greedy birds. Can't stand the sight of them."

"This must be 'a man's thing', to be irritated about small things like seagulls!" James and Andrew looked at each other in understanding.

Back at the house, Ruby excelled herself, turning the little garden into a truly enchanted corner. The multi-coloured bunting and lit up Chinese lanterns did the trick. At the party, everyone kept predicting her a budding career in the world of interior design.

She graciously accepted the compliments, basking in such sudden attention.

"This place is not the same, is it?" Leila fondly pointed out to Maggie.

"Jaw dropping indeed!" Maggie confirmed jovially.

The lemonade and flavoured apple water, which was generously supplied by Venetia, sat in the bowl of ice. Maggie instantly put her seal of approval on it. The two ladies hit it off as two old chums. Leila could not be more pleased. Andrew was on the grill, getting the meat and halloumi kebabs ready to cook.

Finally, David and Greg revealed their surprise. Since Leila didn't let them contribute with the food, instead they hired a hot air balloon ride to finish off the evening.

"If only I could have guessed what you were up to!" Leila shook her head. "I'll get a ride in there even if it's my last one. One has to face one's fears," Leila stated with new found confidence.

James and Ruby were chilling in the hammock, making plans for the rest of the summer holidays. James was also working on his observation skills; from what he could decipher, Greg deep in conversation with Andrew, was discussing the effectiveness of the navy seal tactical G700 flashlights. James was impressed with himself that he had managed to eliminate all the background noise, concentrating on their conversation alone. It seemed that David met his equal, chatting with Ruby's father, not even lip reading was necessary there. James was fairly sure they were talking about the man who sold "the pool chemicals". A wide smile spread across James's face. Maybe he was ready for the next level of secret service induction!

"What are you thinking about right now?" Ruby had to know.

But the feeling, that ascended, was hard to put into words. He was just beyond happy, being surrounded by the genuine people came to care for. It had been a long time since he felt this good. His confidence was budding. He finally found activity that he was keen to develop further and was excited by the idea of further training. He would commit everything to prayer, he had decided. Only God opened up the doors that otherwise would stay shut forever.

"Life is so good right now, that's all."

Ruby had to agree on that too.

At 7 p.m. after a short drive, the party patiently waited to board the hot air balloon. The views promised to be spectacular. The hot air balloon lifted them in turns 500 feet up in the air.

"Look at this view!" Leila could not help exclaiming. The Jurassic coast stretched below.

"Whoa!" All could Ruby say.

"What a liberating feeling! What a view! This is all God doing. I'm thrilled for James," Leila embraced Maggie.

"Can't agree more. But who knows what surprise the Lord yet has for you my darling friend."

Everyone enjoyed the ride immensely. Before everyone knew it, a half an hour ride was over.

"That was a spectacular! Thank you." James approved David and Greg's idea. "A night to remember."

9

Early on Sunday morning, David and Greg picked up both Ruby and James to take them to the Surfer's Church in Newquay. They had to have a head start before the motorway became a Babylonian chaos, with everyone else going places.

"Hi, guys!" David shouted cheerily from the car.

"All ready to go?" Greg greeted them.

"Looking forward to it," Ruby shouted back. What a turn of events this had been. "Wait till my friends hear all that I have to share. Plenty of healthy snacks are packed for the journey; my mother would have a fit if I ate at the service station!" Ruby announced, putting a silky strand of chestnut-brown hair behind her ear.

The time sped up due to thought-provoking conversation and scenic roads. Before they knew it, David was parking near the church building.

"Am I dressed right?" All of a sudden worry hit Ruby.

"I'm sure as long as you have flip flops on and a sun tan, you'll fit in," Greg was trying to keep a straight face.

James squeezed her hand for reassurance. She looked startling in her blue polka dot dress. They headed toward the building and were warmly greeted at the door.

"Welcome!" After all the handshakes, they took their seats promptly.

Ruby looked around in interest. The walls, lined with old surf boards, attracted her attention. Then the band began to play softly. The music was heart-touching. The lyrics of an old hymn poured out as a healing balm: "From all that dwell below the skies, let the Creator's praise arise; let the Redeemer's praise be sung through every land, by every tongue."

Ruby could barely hold the tears back. A welcoming atmosphere was vividly present. Ruby felt that it was not so much the beauty of their voices, but rather the spiritual meaning of the songs which produced an explosion of emotions in her soul.

A pastor, wearing shorts and flip flops, began preaching. He spoke from the Book of John about Jesus becoming a man and living a perfect life in order to die in His prime on behalf of sinners. James was listening, surprised that scholars like Nicodemus still were willing to learn, seeking after Jesus' knowledge.

But what hit him was a new revelation and a clear awareness that God is the One who sees, knows each one, including him. At last James could see how obsessed he was with his own interests, excluding God from his life by insisting that everything had to be done his own way. There was no room for God's wisdom, direction or help in his life. The lights were on! James also realized that the only reason he didn't get it before, when he used to go along to church with his mother, was because his heart and mind weren't open to such truth. Not committing any big sins, not being a criminal like the one they had surveillance on, James lacked the urgency to make things right with God. He wasn't exactly sure what was different but James didn't wish to make the mistake of ignoring God again. *Is God speaking like that to everyone else?* Suddenly aware of the moment when he became so bare and exposed, he questioned, but it was hard to read people's faces.

After the service, refreshments were served. Enjoying freshly brewed coffee, David and Greg couldn't wait to find out what both Ruby and James were thinking and see their first impression.

"What did you both think of the service?"

"I loved the music! The preaching from the Bible was really interesting too." Ruby gave her honest opinion.

"I think God spoke to me like never before. Perhaps because I was prepared to listen this time," James clarified.

"Excellent! Worth the drive then!" David rejoiced.

"I'm not sure why they have to go to such great length to decorate the hall?" James wondered.

"Don't even think of saying that to my mother! She'd love the rustic look here," Ruby came to a defence.

" God suddenly became so real to me. This was the most profound experience I've ever had! To be honest, the band and the surfboards that hung on the walls, all faded away at that moment" shared James, taking a double look around.

"Be careful, music is my haven!" Ruby insisted.

"We, as believers, must be united in spite of all our differences, for example a musical taste! Only this only happens through spiritual growth. " Greg pointed out, acting as a moderator between them.

"I'm pleased for you, mate! This is what both of us have been praying for since we met you," David added.

"So am I. Even though it feels crushing and humbling at the moment!"

"I have to take you out on a concert night when you come for a visit. We are spoilt for choice in Bury St. Edmunds," James hid Greg's point, offering.

"Ok. You are on. It's a deal then."

"God just opened your heart. This is a true miracle. You must read about Lydia and Saul in the Bible. This is exactly what God has done for them and all of us. He always has an initiative." David elaborated further.

"And God is worth it," chimed in Greg. "That first song that they played was written by a poet called Isaac Watts. He lived a very long time ago, but his verses are still sung today. An interesting fact is, as you know I love to read in my spare time, that he fell in love and proposed to a lady called Elizabeth Singer. She was a fellow poet too and was captivated by his verses. They corresponded for some time, but once she met him in person she decided he wasn't attractive enough, declining his offer of marriage. I can imagine tht Isaac must've found it unbearable, but because his Saviour was so precious to him, he served Him all his life. He had an amazingly productive spiritual life, becoming better, not bitter."

"Thank you. This is certainly interesting. Now I want to read about him myself." Ruby approved such a story.

"You'll enjoy it," Greg encouraged her.

Chatting away, all four of them headed towards the car, shaking more hands on the way out.

David asked the pastor to keep them in prayer over the next few days by mentioning about the imminent mission in brief. James gasped at such trust! They knew an effective prayer will happen without explaining everything. The other day he heard David mention a word that described God. *What was it? Omniscient. That's it!* James remembered. All-knowing, the thought of that held power in itself.

"Consider it done. You'll be on our prayer chain. And let me leave you with this Scripture, young man. Isaiah 32:7, 8: 'As for a scoundrel – his devices are evil; he plans wicked schemes to ruin the poor with lying words, even when the plea of the needy is right. But he who is noble plans noble things, and on noble things he stands.' Be courageous!" the pastor encouraged them.

Fully reenergised after lunch, blasting tunes from the new CD that was given to them at the church, they headed off. The traffic was flowing smoothly and listening to meaningful music made the journey less tedious.

"Since it's Sunday, the Day for the Lord, it's right to take a break from work. Tomorrow we will strike, as it is the day we have been waiting for." David sounded edgy already.

"But I have to share with you guys one thing. It totally slipped my mind to say. Remember the sim card that security man sent through you? The minute our experts looked at the data on it, it was obvious what it was about. The man is obsessed with making lists and keeping all the info. We have all his contacts around the world now. Also, the photos of places are top drug growing spots. It is hilarious how the criminals think that they are untouchable, feeling so powerful just for a moment. He openly displayed those photos up at the house. Our field agents will try to get ahead of the game before the drug suppliers are spooked. Also, we got an Intel that the house is heavily armed. The crook has another house in the village of Cinque Terre, Italy. Perhaps he isn't as gullible as we initially thought, always ready for an escape. Not this time though. Therefore, the local military base is sending down trained men with a helicopter for reinforcement. We'll scare the life out of these crooks."

"No way! Is it an Apache by any chance? Apaches are almost impossible to bring down whatever weapon they have up at the house. It also has a twin engine design, if one fails, the other carries the aircraft," James fired away. Never in his life had James had a sense of doing something more worthwhile . This work affected so many lives out there.

"Good insight, but I doubt it. Your teachers will love having you around. Bring Andrew along. He might want to meet our crew at sea!" Greg encouraged him.

If only they could see, what you guys see.

"Yes, sir!" James was eager and ready to help. Would they be able to stop drug growers around the world? That was the next step, surely. Now James began to understand a bit more why David and Greg went to God for help so often.

"Ruby, we are pleased to have you on board too." She sent back a delightful smile through the rear-view mirror.

10

As soon as Ruby walked through the door, her mother couldn't wait to find out what took place at the church.

"Did they push religion down your throat?" Venetia had to know. She impatiently drummed her long fingers on a dining table.

"Mum, if you could only see it for yourself. It was nothing like that," Ruby reassured her. "In fact, you would've loved the interior design there: surf boards all painted in bright colours hanging about the place, giving it a rustic or take-me-back-to-nature look, wide, comfy benches instead of the chairs," Ruby described with a spark in her eyes.

"Really?" was in for a surprise.

"The teaching was the most fascinating part; as though someone told a captivating story about someone very special, a person who knew everything about me. At the same time I didn't have a clue about him. As I was listening, a sense of perfect love that I never knew enveloped me. "

"Ok. You had a positive experience. I give you that. But don't forget that you are in an impressionable stage in life! James, his mother, and the rest of them seem to be very nice people, but I have my reservations. That's all."

Ruby held her tongue. There was no good point infuriating her mother unnecessarily.

Her father, who came in unnoticed, listening for a while, bent to whisper with an element of suspense: "The undercover agents are all right. I had a long chat with them since you had mentioned that I know their suspect and buy pool chemicals from him..."

"Dad! Hush up!" Ruby hissed at him.

"Glad to be of help," there was no stopping him now.

"You are the last person they want the help from, if you shout about it!"

"Ok, ok."

Ruby looked at her phone. No messages. She knew that the lads were meeting to discuss final details today. Not wishing to be excluded or separated from God ever again, she decided to pray. "God, I'm so sorry I've ignored you all these years of my life. Please, forgive me. I want to be your friend. Please help the team to stop this evil. I ask in Jesus' most precious and wonderful name." Unburdened, she felt peace and deep joy that she didn't have a solid reason for. Ruby never felt like it. She knew now that God, who created everything, desired to be her friend for eternity. Why her parents never go to church? She suspected it would not be easy to convince them, but it was in God's hands now, perhaps also in her prayer.

The text message came, as though waiting for the importance of the moment to sink in. "When r u free? Speak soon, J. X"

Remembering what the pastor quoted on Sunday, she sent a reply: "If the Son sets you free, you will be free indeed."

"Que?" James could not help but mimic his favourite character from Faulty Towers.

"I do believe in God. I'm a Christian now. What do u reckon?"

"No way!!! Be at yours in 5 secs."

"OK."

Barely stepping through the door, James squeezed her so tight that she had to say: "Ouchy!"

"I'm so thrilled for you. How did it happened? I must know everything!"

"Me too," she smiled back. They stood still for a moment, grinning silly at each other. Then Ruby offered James to share his part of the story first.

"You know, when God met me right there, at the church, I came home and began to pray, asking for forgiveness of my sins. This made me realise that I also must forgive my father. So I did. The anger towards him was lifted. I can't even explain how good that felt, it is gone!"

"Incredible…" was all Ruby could say.

"Back to the apprehension of the drug dealer… when is it happening?" She was half whispering to him.

"You go first. Your news is more exciting." James would not let her off the hook until he heard everything. Ruby described how she was feeling at the church, her thinking ever since, feeling unresolved since she had heard the good news. Finally she wanted to help so bad, realizing that by praying she could be most useful. Not rocket science – it just took her fifteen years to realize that she needed God's help in her life.

"Back to you now," Ruby was impatient.

"The team is on alert now! The decision is made to move in on him tomorrow tonight. The operation is on. According to surveillance, the owner is planning some sort of a get together up at his mansion. A perfect chance to get him and the gang all at the same time!"

Ruby had not seen James so animated since she had met him.

"Wow! What are we going to do?"

"You, Andrew and I will have a super duper role, doing some … babysitting," James let it out.

"Are you kidding ?" Ruby wouldn't compete with the Royal Marines, but it came as such a shock.

"Remember, I'm a bit of a hero to the mother and with the kids now. hope it will help. We'll have to stay with them and keep them calm. I expect this will be a hard blow to them. Not sure whether the wife knows what her husband is really up to."

"Ok, I'm up for that. Let have a practice. How many games do you know?"

"A few. I have a five year old cousin, did I tell you that?" James added.

The next morning, James was to wait for the final text from David before he and Ruby were to head out towards "Mr. Bugsworth's vertiginous mansion", as James called it. It was not a massive hill, but unless he was on his scooter, it would take some time to climb it.

Both he and Ruby sat down for a quick prayer. God's protection was vital as reality sank in. James couldn't predict how everything would go tonight, but he hoped that God had their backs.

His phone rang as soon as they were done praying.

"Yes, we're on our way!" James promptly informed.

"Are we going yet?"

"Yes, now!"

They jumped on their scooters with James in a lead.

As promised a helicopter was sent from Middle Wallop with a team of trained men. DASCU combined their efforts with the army, receiving more help than expected. The helicopter flew low over the Sandbanks, almost touching the tops of the sky reaching pine trees. The village had never seen such excitement. Most of the city residents, who escaped for a bit of quiet, were about to be disturbed tonight. Apparently, according to David, peace and quiet in the neighbourhood was pre-empted for an order "to uproot the evil of drug dealing with effective results."

The war on drugs had been declared tonight.

At the electronic gates, the black-suited security was replaced by a police officer. He let James and Ruby right through. The feeling that they were part of this apprehension was indescribable. The mansion was buzzing with the armed police. Even before they reached the front door, the loudest wailing had reached them.

"Oh, oh, I didn't know. Not a clue! How can he do this to us? Aaahh, aaahh, aaahhh." A female voice was echoing through the entire neighbourhood. All visible pride and pretence that James had spotted at the first glance at Mrs. Bugsworth vanished entirely now. Ruby was wondering where the kids were. She asked the armed officer who was guarding the front door. He pointed her towards the stairs. Ready to go up, James spotted a few men in Tom Ford's costumes, handcuffed. Their immaculate suits were not the only resemblance they had now. James was sure one of them was the host, but it was hard to tell who was who. Everyone wore the same mask of misery. A sour bunch indeed. They didn't even have a chance to put up a fight or use their sophisticated weapons or security men who were on the floor now. If James didn't know better, he almost could have felt sorry for them. Ruby ran up the stairs. A little girl was sitting on her bed, unaware of her mother's turmoil, while the boy was glued to the window.

"What are those?" he asked Ruby as soon as he saw her.

"It's an army helicopter to help us fight people who make wrong choices."

"Is that an apache?" Thinking hard about something else, the boy asked again. "Did my dad make a wrong choice?" his eyes, as two big saucers, were staring back at them.

"Sadly, yes, but anyone can change, if they really think about it and are sorry enough," explained Ruby feeling heartbroken for the kid.

"An Apache would make more noise and dust than this one," explained James, joining them upstairs. "It also has two engines."

"When I grow up, I want to be a pilot," plainly stated the boy.

"That's really impressive. You must do really well in school," reassured Ruby.

She looked at the girl who appeared so very sad. "Would you like to see the most adorable Dalmatian dogs?" Her face lit up instantly. She nodded. "Tomorrow. Have a good sleep now."

From that point everything happened quickly and when the commotion settled the helicopter flew back to its base at Middle Wallop. The children were safely tucked in bed in a different house, soothed by a few drops of lavender oil that Ruby had managed to find.

"Lavender will put you to sleep like nothing else!" Ruby pointed out seeing James's enquiring look.

The DASCU agents had Mr. Bugsworth and his gang in a custody, taking them straight to the local police station in Bournemouth. The security there was doubled.

Everyone except the agents who promised to join them once formalities were over, headed towards the Plantation Pub. The lights hung between the tall trees. Jazz notes flowed in the background. Night fell, but it was still pleasantly warm.

Andrew shared some of the details over the drinks. Apparently there was a speed escape boat that was ready and waiting to depart at a moment's notice. The Royal Marines using their Rigid Raider dealt with that effectively. Andrew was invited for a ride, which was a dream come true. The mansion was sealed. All the computers and documents were confiscated. The family was going home tomorrow and a police investigation would begin regarding the drug dealers.

David and Greg joined the civilian celebration party. "Thank you all for your support and encouragement!" David began to clap. Everyone joined in.

"Apprehension like this one is extremely effective. Hopefully it is a good lesson for the rest of the criminals, especially since everything will be in the newspapers. All those involved will get what's coming to them."

At this point James's phone started to ring. The name on the screen flashed "Dad". James swallowed and pressed answer.

"Hi, Son! How's it going? How's your summer break so far?" his voice was pleading. James hadn't heard from him in a while now.

"Hi, Dad! I'm good. The holidays have never been better." James was surprised how easy the words came out. This change was for real.

Then James suddenly recalled a scene with the dead man on the beach. He knew he had to see his father soon and, as one waterman to another, he owed him the truth. Once he was freed from hatred, there was enough room for other emotions. He felt sorry for his dad, that selfishness like a seaweed tangled up everything that was important is his heart. James had extra compassion and it was growing on him.

"And how is everything with you? Are you still in Puerto Escondido?" James asked.

"Yes, that's right. You would not believe the weather here. Scorching, but not too bad near the ocean I suppose."

"I'd love to visit you."

"That would be super, Son! Let's plan it."

"I'm up for it. Have to get a paper round and start saving."

"Ok. That's a plan," his dad encouraged the idea.

"Speak to you soon. It was really good to hear your voice." James really meant it.

"The same here. Speak soon." There was a pause, then his father added. "I've missed you."

"Ok, Dad, speak to you soon. Bye."

James wished nothing more but to share with his father the real truth about himself and God. His newfound forgiveness and unconditional love through Christ felt so liberating. After all, his surfer father, walking on the edge of death daily needed this spiritual insight the most. How could his dad face eternity on his own? After finishing their conversation, he knew he had to give it over to prayer first. By watching the police at work, James knew that if he didn't get serious about prayer time, he would be like a man who runs but not trains. He had learnt that lesson all right. However, a more imminent thing was just on his mind.

The music, playing in the background, suddenly slowed. While all the adults went to get a pint, James decided to seize his chance. Ruby stood there, looking enchanting. Her hair clasped in a ponytail. The dress she wore was the best James had seen so far. Flowery and bright coloured, it suited her complexion very much.

"Young lady, will you do me the honour of dancing with me?" The line sounded as though practiced or memorized perfectly.

"Would love to." Ruby placed her hand into his, with James leading her to the centre of the outdoor dancing area.

Walking hand in hand, James whispered into her ear: "How epic it is that we've met!" Ruby nodded, agreeing.

An invisible, but all powerful God, having only the very best to offer, was orchestrating every detail of their lives.

Part Two:

In the Streamline

Not to have any drag while paddling, to take the path that will be of least resistance.

11

rent was up before dawn. Anticipating a pleasantly
familiar drive from La Punta to catch some waves
at Zicatela Beach, he moved as fireman responding
to the alarm. After a quick glass of banana smoothie, he
reached his car in less than three minutes. The best surf
happened early. Trent secured his board onto a roof rack,
hoping to be at the beach first. Driving out, he knew he
would never get tired of Mexico. Being here was like landing
in another world. The constant bright sun made the clear
milky-blue sky look larger. Its glare was so strong that
sunglasses were not a fashionable item, but a must. The
green foliage was lavish. The dusty, red dirt roads gave way

to pavement nearer to the beach. The colourful, unusual looking birds and wild orchids in their unrivalled beauty reminded that there was paradise once. The surfing community at La Punta was everything he hoped for: close-knit, one in spirit, embracing. But the ocean was the magnet that always pulled him the most. Living on the edge is what Trent craved as bad as the oxygen.

Gripping the steering wheel, another pleasant day lay ahead of him, but a pang of regret rose out of blue. The feeling that something might rock his usual routine was growing inside him. Like a storm, raging in the depth of the ocean, not obvious, but confirmed by the high waves that hit the shore later. On the surface everything looked just the same: towering palm trees semi circling the beach, endless stretch of white sand, terracotta roofs of the beach cafes always beckoning the tourists. The birds were insistently cruising above the waves in a pack. Yet Trent shivered, superstitiously touching his tattoo. He tried hard to detach himself from this feeling; brushing it aside, Trent refocused, hoping to rip the biggest waves today. When he first arrived here he started off at Carrizalillo Beach for beginners. After a few years he found himself among the Zicatela's elite surfers. Such a fact cleared the last cobwebs of doubt. Great surfers weren't made sitting on the beach, thinking too much. This spot was just as perfect as when he first saw it in a photo in a surfing magazine back in England.

Trent observed the ocean for a moment. The long, high waves teasing the bravest to challenge them. His muscles, toned to perfection due to daily surfing, were itching for action. His pale skin was long gone, along with his brown hair, which was now starkly bleached by the intensity of the sun. With a longboard under his arm he headed down to the beach, breathing in the salt-scented air.

"Hola, mi amigo!" An old man, a regular observer, greeted him.

"Hola! Que buena dia!" he replied. "Another perfect day!"

"Si. There is nowhere else like Mexico," the man nodded. Aztec soup is on the menu today."

"Excellent! Gracias."

Walking on burning sand, Trent suddenly had a flashback to a family holiday in Cornwall, his son James, still a toddler. The English beach had been deserted at the end of September. Trent, eager to check out the waves, popped into a surf shop.

"How's the water?" he had wondered aloud.

"It's tropical today, mate. No need for hat or booties."

Thinking about it now, he felt bittersweet. Comparing this place to the other, Trent now tasted what was truly tropical daily. Yes, all right, it came at a price. But leaving his family behind had seemed the only option when the surf had called him. Now, out of guilt, he didn't dwell on how they were getting on without him. He immersed himself into the surf world; swimming, going to the Breath Hold Survival course, few hours of sleep to be up for 5am daily. Life was conveniently simple, no room for emotions. If only he could permanently shake this growing unease. Trent was annoyed, ready to channel it against the teasing waves.

Jovially greeting his mates, Trent fearlessly paddled out, his body pressed to his board. The most dedicated were already in the water. Determined to be close to the best wave, he positioned himself in the centre of the board. Waiting for a perfect moment, he shouted a loud "left!" Trent ripped from the peak of the wave and propelled himself into a barrel. The mass of water just carried him in. The words of Laird Hamilton, his role model, echoed true: "To take on forces of nature, that's when you feel most alive!" As the waves subserviently obeyed him, conquering them for a moment made him feel in control. Trent liked that a lot. All the hard work he put into his talent for surfing, paid off generously. There were always new manoeuvres to learn, bigger waves to catch. The possibilities in the water were infinite. The ocean was never boring or predictable. Trent tasted freedom as he did salty water, feeling as alive as he ever did.

A few hours flew by until hunger pulled Trent out of the water. A shady palapa stood there as a refuge, ready to give a deserved break.

"Momentito! What's today's special, por favor?" Trent inquired in fluent Spanish.

"Seafood." A super fit waiter cheekily flashed his teeth.

"One seafood platter, please! And an Aztec soup."

The octopus was tender and succulent, nothing like the rubbery version he had tried back home. The Aztec soup created an explosion of flavours. No wonder it was pricey.

While eating, Trent was surprised by the nagging thought that he needed to go and visit Jose. He might control the waves, but his emotions were out of their usual order, no doubt. The urgency would not leave him. Jose was the one who taught him Spanish when he first arrived, such a good friend. Since Trent had begun surfing, most days he hardly saw the man.

This would be a trek since Jose lived inland. Trent didn't feel an appeal to get away from the water even for a day, but he owed him one! All those long hours in the evenings spent in learning Spanish verbs and phrases. Jose was a real deal. To forget about him entirely would be unforgivable. He made up his mind to go.

With air-conditioning on full blast, Trent didn't even bother with the satnav. He was driving towards the mountains, a place still unreached by technology. The locals didn't know what they were missing. Knowing the road, his jeep was the suitable car for such a journey. Trent only hoped Jose's village had electricity by now. After buying a few bars of chocolate and beer for later, Trent drove on. The journey seemed shorter since he knew the roads better. At last Trent spotted Jose puttering outside.

"Hola, amigocho!"

"Hola, old friend!" Jose was beaming from ear to ear. "What a surprise! I've almost lost hope of seeing you again. The time crawls over here on the outskirts of civilization as the young call it," he heartily laughed. Jose grabbed Trent's hand with much strength, embracing him. Trent didn't even bother to protest. The stiffness of a Brit was long gone, replaced by the affectionate warmth of the locals.

"I could never forget you! After all you've done for me since I first arrived! Do I dare ask if there is any electricity yet? I bought us some beer."

"What's wrong with the good old cellar, young man? Yes, for beer; no, for electricity," Jose chuckled. "We are blessed, with electricity or not."

The word *blessed* shot through Trent as an electric shock. He had a good look around. Piles of wood, dug out dirt spread near an unfinished well. His friend was getting older, but the work only mounted up. What kind of a blessing was there around here?

Touched by the man's strength not to surrender to the harshness of life or his age, Trent offered. "Can I be of any help?"

"In fact, you can. I'm in the middle of building a well. I could do with an extra pair of hands. The well digger has taken ill. You can see we made a big mess and little progress so far!"

Trent rolled up his sleeves. "Sounds good. We must work for our beers then. What do you want me to do?!"

"How about you lower me by the rope into the well? I will dig and you empty the buckets?"

"Don't you have a ladder?" Trent wondered.

"Si. What am I thinking, old fool? Your visit is timely. Dry season is the best time to dig." Armed with the ladder, chisel and mallet, they began on the work.

"Terrific! I knew surfing was overrated." Both of them burst out laughing. The old friendship rekindled in no time. Trent never understood how he could not talk for years with a man and pick up where they left off. If only this was true of Leila…. Brushing the thought away, like sweat from his brow, he focused on giving his friend a hand.

In spite of the man's age, Trent was impressed how much progress Jose made below. He steadily passed the buckets of dirt up. It looked like he needed company to encourage him to do it more than anything else. The job will be done in a few hours.

"How are you doing my friend? Tired yet?"

"Me? You got to be kidding! I can last for hours. As long as we keep drinking water, no problem. Keep going! You will see. People from town are just as hard working!" Trent reassured him.

"Bueno. If you are good, I'm good!"

The words barely trailed off his tongue as the ground shifted. Again and again, with more force each time. There was no mistake about it: an earthquake was happening.

The ground, mixed with the rock, began falling down into the well, with Jose at the bottom.

Everything happened too fast. Unable to stop the disaster, Trent panicked. At sea, he could always paddle harder, swim longer underwater. This earthquake shook not only the ground, but his confidence to the core.

"Jose, are you there?" terrified, he shouted into the deep hole.

"Si," a faint answer travelled back.

"Are you injured?"

"Si. I'm wedged between the wooden poles. Can't move. I'm buried in," a weak voice came up.

"I'll see what I can do. Just hold on, old man!"

Trent paced up and down, unable to get any signal on his phone. Frustrated, he threw it on the ground. Fear was rising out of the pit of his stomach. *What can I do now?*

Pulling his hair with both hands, he continued pacing.

There was no one for miles around. Should he start the car and pull the logs out?

"Trent, mi amigo! Listen carefully. I have peace with God. Don't worry too much about me."

The old Mexican began to mumble something while Trent frantically dug the wood out of the way, making his way to Jose with his bare hands.

"I'm going to dig you out no matter what. Just hang in there!"

The man's faint voice became bolder. A few words sounded familiar: "Senior, por favor, no me dejes ni me abandones…" Trent had no time to figure out why and what the man was muttering.

Something beyond human energy filled him, releasing every reserve of stored up energy to rescue his friend before it was too late.

12

Autumn had arrived on time as it always did. James was baffled about who in their right mind would be looking forward to the start of school? There were plenty of studious pupils on the Net giving advice about how to get the best marks. James, on the other hand, felt apprehensive about starting year eleven, his GCSE year. The mock exams were a sheer nightmare. Still riding on the waves of his adventure in Dorset and feeling nostalgic, James avoided looking at the dates. It was like a bomb on a timer. The sixth of September was just a few days away, his official start of the school year. One thing instantly brightened his mood though. Ruby was only a Snapchat away. Thinking of his new friends, James's heart swelled with warmth. He began putting together his school bag: scientific calculator, a pencil case, markers and a water bottle.

On Tuesday his alarm confirmed that going to school was an undeniable fact. *Might as well get on with it.* The minute his mind computed such information, he leaped out of bed. James was first at the car; Leila was searching for the keys.

"I'll be a minute!" She said, rushing back inside.

"Ok. We have time, mum!" James was pleased that he had time to text Ruby. "All the best for today! Thinking of you. Talk soon, J."

Driving off at last, he could not wait to see Phil, his best mate, to share what happened over the summer.

In the middle of the courtyard a rowdy group of students were getting excited. James couldn't see what exactly was happening. Pushing through the crowd slowly, he finally got a glimpse. One of the new Y7 boys was being pushed about.

"Where did you get your 'posh shoes'? Wait. Don't tell me. I know: Barnardo's or Oxfam, yeah?

A short boy, with a mass of black curly hair, smugly acted as the ring leader. His mocking attitude rubbed off on the others. The crowd enflamed the mockery. Someone else started pulling his school bag off.

As a rule James wouldn't get involved. That would be placing a bullseye on his back forever. Hoping for more boldness lately, this looked like an opportunity to step up. After a deep breath, muttering, "God, help me" he plunged himself forward, right next to the boy. There was no time to come up with an elaborate plan.

"Guys! Listen up. Didn't you all know? His mother and father were in a car crash. His old aunt took him in. The head master will put you in isolation if you mess with him." A deep silence fell. Such a sober reminder did the trick. Everyone froze, the mob atmosphere bursting. The crowd grudgingly began to leave.

"I'm James by the way. I hope you don't mind me interrupting this riot. Sorry for making up a sad story, couldn't think of anything else at the time." James faced the year seven boy. The courage of the moment came out of nowhere. James could hardly believe that he was doing it.

The boy looked up, shaken, but with immense gratitude in his eyes. However, he didn't say a word.

The ring leader spat in disgust right next to James. With nothing else to say, he followed the rest.

James, seeing how shaken up the boy was, made sure that he safely entered his classroom. Then he rushed off to his own. All the mobiles had to be switched off during lessons, which was really annoying. What if Greg or David urgently had to get in contact with him? May be he could get a special arrangement. He'd have to look into it.

The rest of the day passed uneventful. There were a few new teachers to meet, then a short lunch break. That was by far the best part of the day. James didn't like the last or the first days of school when not much was happening. Watching Phil, eating his sandwich at break, James pressed on with his tale. His friend nearly lost half of his sandwich once James mentioned that he was involved with the DASCU.

"Unreal, mate, unreal! How did you pull that off?" was all Phil could say, astounded.

"Being at the right place, at the right time. It just happened…. I suppose." James felt uncomfortable, but could not help it. The courage that he had earlier simply evaporated. He could not bring himself to break to his friend that he became a Christian. This could cause a real stir in their friendship. What if Phil thought he was weird? Then what? Who will he play Xbox with or hang out after school? The old fear sank its claws with new ferociousness.

"You're so lucky! See you after the lessons."

"I guess. See ya!" James's face felt as though set on fire.

At the end of the day James and Phil left school together. James kept looking out for the year seven, but couldn't see him anywhere. James promised to keep Phil in the loop if anything else developed with DASCU. But the part about his faith still was somehow a challenge to break out.

"Shall we go to mine and play on Xbox for a bit?" offered James.

"Cool. Let's go."

At home, James grabbed a snack and they started playing a game on his console. He felt distracted though. For once his favourite skateboarding game could not capture his attention. Had the summer break changed him that much? Thoughts about his dad troubled him. He would love to see him but when and how?

A phone call from Ruby broke the troubling thoughts.

"Hi!"

"Hi there! How'd it go in school today?"

"Good. Something really weird happened though. I certainly scored on 'the most exciting summer break' contest," She proudly announced.

"At first they thought I was so bored that I made it all up. We had such a laugh. Everybody sounded jealous of me once I convinced them it did happen. And how was your first day back?"

"Oh, someone was being bullied. I had to get involved."

"Well done! Who was bullied?"

"Someone new. I've never done anything remotely the same before. I prayed and went for it." James was surprised how easy it was to talk to Ruby and acknowledge God's involvement in his life.

"Every experience like that is a character builder."

"Ruby, you are wiser beyond your years!" James was only happy to comment. They both burst out in laughter.

***

The first few weeks at school went smoothly. James finally got into his routine. He and Ruby were chatting daily. All seemed to be back to normal.

On Wednesday afternoon, as he and Phil were playing on the Xbox, James got a text from Greg.

"Need to talk soon. When is good for u? G."

"Carry on. I'll be back in a sec." Walking out to the kitchen, James dialled Greg's number.

"What's up, mate?" James was burning up with much interest alredy.

"Good to hear your voice, seems like forever since I saw you last!"

"Tell me about it. Time crawls when you're in school."

"No fear! Half term is coming up soon. Are you looking forward to it?"

"Yeah. What a question!"

"Any plans yet?"

"I'm hoping to visit Ruby."

"Because of our recommendation, they put you on a recruitment program. How does that sound?" Greg aimed at the core of the matter.

James gasped. "This is the best news ever. I'm in."

"Didn't you say that you're learning Spanish? How's it going?"

"Since Dad went off travelling I've always wanted to go and see him. He's surfing in Mexico I think. I have a Spanish tutor once a week. He is pleased with my progress."

"David and I are heading to Mexico at the end of October." There was a pause. Greg gave James time for the news to sink in. "If you're up for it, you just got yourself a seat on the plane. You can interpret for us. We'll be heading to Oaxaca. Expenses are covered."

"No way! For real? Did you know my father lives in Puerto Escondido…." James couldn't believe the coincidence.

"Is that a *yes* then?"

"More than a yes!" he squealed with glee.

"Talk soon."

"Can't wait. Bye."

As the conversation ended, James continued to absorb the news. Now he definitely would be counting the minutes till October half term. All of a sudden his life was in the streamline of God's favour he just knew it. Feeling so guilty for being embarrassed of his faith, he purposed to do something about it. But there was an issue of his promise to visit Ruby. How would he break the news to her?

"I'm off. Have to start on homework. Will catch you tomorrow," Phil shouted through the door.

"Sorry, mate. See you tomorrow." As the door shut behind his friend, James relaxed. He better ask God to have more guts. If he was scared to talk to Phil how on earth would he be able to talk to his father about God? "I will not be a coward!" James said aloud.

After dinner, James flew up the stairs to his study desk. He decided to pull the trigger and talk to Ruby, hoping she would understand. If he kept thinking about it, the unknown would drive him crazy.

He sent her a text: "R u free to talk?"

"Ok." The reply came in a flash.

"Hey!" Ruby answered in her melodic voice.

"Hi! How are things?"

"Really good. And with you?"

"I have some awesome news to share. The thing is Greg and David are heading to Mexico. They offered for me to be their interpreter. You know that's where my dad lives now?"

The silence was deafening.

"Ruby, are you there? Do you mind at all?"

"Of course not!" she spoke at last, in a voice contradicting her words. "Who could say no to an offer like that? I'm really pleased for you. I better go. I have so much homework already. Better get on with it. Nice to catch up with you."

"Ok. I really appreciate that you understand it. Speak soon."

"Bye."

Even though there was nothing to alert James in Ruby's words, he sensed a detachment. Ruby didn't sound her usual self. This was bothersome, but James didn't want to be paranoid.

Back in her room, Ruby sat quiet. Then she curled herself in a ball and started crying. However, a bit later, she was dialling her phone with firm resolve.

13

The buzz of the phone returned Leila to the here and now. She could barely rise from her knees. Looking at her watch, she realized that she just spent an hour in prayer. Was that even possible?

The screen displayed "Ruby".

"Oh, hi! Aren't you in school, darling?"

"I'm on a break. I needed to chat with someone who would share my excitement. I've enrolled in a vocal course at 'In the Round' in London for half term."

"What an amazing opportunity, Ruby. You'll learn a lot and enjoy it immensely. Remember everything that we talked about for establishing your voice."

"Yeah. I will," Ruby whispered softly.

"You don't sound excited," Leila pointed out.

"A few things are on my mind at the moment. I'm sure I will once I'm there. I gotta run. Bye."

Leila looked at the silent phone, not sure what just happened. This was not the Ruby she knew. Puzzled, slowly she put the phone down. Good thing God always knows what is happening. She could commit Ruby to Him. It felt liberating to off load her dearest and nearest to someone with much more power than her own.

Later on James pushed through the door, landing on the sofa while his bag, in one well aimed shot reached the bottom of the stairs.

"All right? How was your day, darling?"

"Not bad at all. And yours?"

"Marvellous. Chatted with Maggie, which was encouraging. Also Ruby told me she's going up to London for half term. Do you know anything about it?"

"Nope." His quick reply spoke volumes to Leila.

"I'm sure it's not a big deal. She'll tell you in her time." Leila simplified the case. She didn't want to press for an explanation just yet.

"I thought it would be good to pray over your trip tonight. What do you think? I'm not sure what I achieved today but decided we'll go out for Mexican. So you could compare the food, will see if they know what they are doing over there."

"Great, Mum." James approved.

"Good. One problem solved then."

They sat in the lounge sipping on a cordial that Leila recently discovered: chilled coconut water mixed with fizzy mineral water. James stretched his legs, which had gotten even longer over the summer.

"So how are Maggie and Andrew?" James inquired with interest.

"All right."

"I really miss Andrew." He admitted frankly.

"What about your dad? How much do you remember of him?" Leila tested the water. James, sitting opposite, was the image of his father at his teens. She remembered looking through the family photos at Trent's house many times: lanky, with unruly brown and with slightly crooked teeth on the bottom which made his smile so unique. The, her heart with new resolve longed for her husband.

"Not sure. He left so long ago. He's a faint memory now."

"I was telling Maggie earlier how I've learnt so much from tennis lessons. Skills and knowledge are powerful. I know that this trip seemed to come out of blue. But even a good fireman will not send his partner unprepared into the fire. God is doing His work. He was working on our behalf. We must pray that He will give us both His unconditional love for your father. Often only then the most remarkable happens. God must be working on your father too. He doesn't need a flight to Mexico."

"Mum, you are spot on. I can use the power of prayer. I just need more courage to tell friends about my faith."

"Darling, nothing happens overnight. Just be patient and trust God."

Leila closed her eyes, sitting still for a moment. Then she began "Holy and eternal God. We worship and praise you. Your goodness is overwhelming towards us, sinners. We humbly come, asking you to forgive us. Please help us to obey you daily." His mother had such a way with words. But her sincerity and closeness with God touched his heart deeply. He knew that she spent considerable amount of time in prayer every day. When she prayed, it was obvious that she knew God intimately. She continued: "Fill us with your unconditional love. We don't have it in ourselves. Please help us to love others as you love them. In the name of your Son, Jesus Christ, Amen."

"Amen. Thanks, Mum. I better get ready. Look forward to the Mexican." James already was speeding up the staircase.

"Yeah, me too. I looked the restaurant up. They do a lot of charity by feeding street kids in Mexico City. If the food isn't that great, at least we did something right by eating there."

14

fter that life-altering phone call from Greg, James could not think about anything but Mexico. He Googled the images of Oaxaca on the internet once more. There were pages of tropical trees and houses, painted in unique to Mexico colours. But to inhale the sea and mountain air, and to walk the streets, taking in the local atmosphere, would be entirely different. If only time moved faster. James religiously checked the weather in Puerto Escondido. He learnt that October was turtle nesting time. Imagine that. He also had to break the news to his dad soon. James daydreamed about it, pretending to be interested in the lessons. What was his father doing right now? What was he like? Will they get on? The only way to answer those questions would be to go and check everything out for himself. Sadly, James had another eighteen days to go before he could do that. Time crawled these days.

"Mum, listen to this. I was reading up on turtles nesting near Puerto Escondido. Fascinating!" James walked into the kitchen, interrupting everything Leila was doing, pouring his enthusiasm out.

"Olive Ridley sea turtles emerge from the surf. They navigate a complex migratory route over 1000 miles of ocean (without visual landmarks) to lay their eggs on the beach where they were born. Escobilla Beach, in the state of Oaxaca is where they nest. Imagine that? And how can such intelligent creatures just evolve all by themselves? They must have always been this way. And here I'm wondering who is more scared me or the grass snake when I lift the compost lid off? It knows my presence and slithers away! At first I was so scared, but realized that it was more scared of me. The theory of evolution never suited me while in school,"

Leila agreed.

"Someone more intelligent must have made them!" James stated. "I do hope the snakes in Oaxaca are just as timid!"

***

Back in Mexico, Trent sat, with his hands still shaky. He had no energy to walk now that the adrenaline rush had gone. Good thing he had planned to stay overnight. No way could he be driving in such a state. Jose was resting on his bed, propped up with pillows. A jar of tequila sat by his side. Trent needed a blue cactus drink tonight. He understood that Jose just wanted to rest. He disliked going to the doctors himself. Hardly anyone got sick over here: what bacteria was not burnt by the sun, was finished off by tequila. But there was not a cure against the storms, tropical rains, poisonous spiders or earthquakes as it proved today.

As the night fell, everything went pitch black outside. Only the stars gave light, looking closer than anywhere else he had been. Though exhausted, Trent could not imagine going to bed. He had to be vigilant, making sure Jose was all right. Gazing at the stars, sipping his tequila, the knowledge of how insignificant his life was compared to the vast universe, struck him. *Maybe feeling uneasy was a warning?* He wondered out of sheer superstition. As the drink relaxed him, he could not fight the sleep in spite of his best intentions to watch the old man. The sweat was pouring off his forehead. Awake at last, his body felt stiff from sitting down all night. Trent stood up. Stretching and quickly wiping the sweat at the same time, he rushed to check on Jose. The man looked beaten up, but perky. Nothing wrong with the broad, content smile that he displayed.

"Amigo, I wish I could do something to express my gratitude. Did you rest well?" the old man asked.

"Not really. I dreamt that I was out in the ocean, alone with the power of towering waves up against me. I tried to surf, but my board was snapped in half. Gasping for air, it had felt like the waves were after me, conspiring to get me and bury me in the depth of the ocean. I kept fighting them, but then I heard laughter from above and I was pushed to the bottom of the ocean."

"Sounds nearly as bad as the earthquake. You are in my prayers." Jose gave a promise from his bed.

"Is there any family that can look after you?"

"Si. Can you get a piece of paper from the drawer over there, please? My nephew was going to visit. Perhaps he can come today. You can go home and rest."

Trent assured that there was no rush for him to leave. The phone still didn't have any reception.

The early morning was already getting hot. The majestic mountains stood in contrast to the bright sun as if nothing had happened. Yet Trent felt troubled. What if Jose died last night? How could he live with himself? What if his dream was a reality and he died himself? These were pestering, mosquito-like questions.

After they ate, a truck pulled up. It was his nephew arriving just in time. As he was pulling in, it dawned on Trent that his old friend might not be spared from troubles, but he was looked after. This was a true blessing, he would give him that.

The drive home seemed shorter, even though he stopped by the side of the road for a pork taco. As he was about to park, he saw a crowd of people standing outside. He wouldn't be surprised if it were in town. Mexicans had plenty of time to stand and talk as they pleased. This was a typical occurrence. What surprised him was that they stood in the middle of the car park of his apartment. This was unusual, in the heat of the day.

Rolling down the window, he shouted, "Anything the matter?"

"Don't you know? The whole block of flats burnt down last night," someone shouted out. Trent could hardly believe his ears. "Donde?"

"On Playa Street." Trent's heart skipped a beat. This was his street. He parked the best he could and pushed himself through the crowd. The sight that opened up to his eyes was a devastating one. The whole row of apartments was wiped out, only black smoke still rising. He knew better. One of those flats was where he rented.

The observers chatted with much excitement, discussing the latest details of the fire in urgency. Apparently some electrical wires were old and faulty. One of the flats started the whole fire. Compensation was promised, but Trent didn't hold his breath about it. He felt crushed about all his belongings being wiped out like that. He sat on the side of the road with his head in his hands. Shortly, a fairly tall, well-built man with a broad, sincere smile approached him.

"Hi, you must be one of the tenants here, are you? I'm John. I volunteer as a chaplain at the fire station here, came out here from San Diego."

"Unfortunately for me, yes. Nice to meet you. I'm a Brit."

They shook hands. Trent at once felt at ease with this trustworthy man.

"Do you live here? Have you lost your stuff?"

"Yes. And everything I own. I was blessed my documents and surf boards were with me." Now he finally understood why Jose used such a word. It seemed the most fitting in such circumstances, reassuring and comforting. The knowledge that someone more powerful than nature and circumstances was watching over him became vital as air.

"Phew! One good thing I suppose. The firefighters arrived promptly on the fire scene. They did their very best. At times it is a losing battle."

"Not sure what I'll do now. I have no family or friends out here. Just a few acquaintances. I should head down to the beach and see what's for rent."

"You're welcome to stay with my family. Please, consider it. You would be more than welcome," John was insistent.

At first Trent was taken aback by such offer. He stood motionless. The simple kindness of a stranger seemed too much. But as his mother would always say, beggars can't be choosers. At this desperate moment such an act of compassion was overwhelming.

"Thank you. I'll happily take you up on the offer." It was no brainer what to answer.

John made you feel like you have always known him. His wife, Valerie, with a dazzling, celebrity type smile, also made you feel at home.

"Anything to eat or drink, Trent? Please make yourself at home."

They had three young children who curiously looked at Trent, but carried on playing.

"Do you have any children?" Valerie caught him off guard.

"Yes. I have a son. He's fifteen. Wait a minute, must be sixteen already."

"When did you see him last?" Trent was surprised how the question made him more depressed than the news of the fire.

"A few years ago." Trent felt his face reddening.

"Oh. You must miss him very much." Valerie burst out her compassion onto him.

"I do. But it's only my fault," his voice trembled. Swallowing hard he explained: "We've started to talk on the phone not long ago. It has been really good to hear from him."

The inner beauty that Valerie possessed made him wonder what instant impression he made on others. Beauty ran much deeper than tan and muscles he could see that now, comparing himself to such a lady. Surely he must appear to others as he really was: selfish, egocentric, emotionless. *Who would leave his own flesh and blood?* His thoughts shifted a gear suddenly. The events of the past 24 hours dramatically sealed his views on life and death, crashing harder than any wave he ever surfed.

"We're about to eat. I hope you're hungry." A tempting offer returned Trent back to reality.

"I'd love to join you. Thank you."

"Do you mind if we say a blessing on the meal?" John stated rather than asked.

"Go ahead. Don't mind me."

John bowed his head and said a short, but heartfelt prayer. Trent was handed a plate with four appetizing looking tacos. Valerie pointed out that tacos de Papa is mainly potatoes. The spices made this dish stand out from any potatoes Trent had ever tasted. He knew nothing about this family, but their attitude towards him instantly made him feel as though he was accepted as he was.

Around eight p.m. his mobile rang. Trent couldn't believe his own ears listening to James. The day was finishing better than he expected. Now he would have to check with John for permission to invite James to stay. Finally his son was making his way to meet him and here we was: homeless. If there was a God, He knew how to humble him once and for all. At this point he didn't mind or was surprised any more. The knowledge that something of immense proportions was absent from his life dawned on him. This new circle of people gathered around him was so different to the surfing crowd. *But why, all of a sudden, was his life being turned upside-down*, he wondered? He would kill for the right answers.

15

The idea to enrol in a vocal course in London came to Ruby out of nowhere. Or so it seemed. A few days ago she overheard her mother talking about Sophie, her best friend from school, who lived in the city.

"She thinks she has made it. I was hoping she would come for a visit this summer, but no! Her loss. What is there to do in the city during summer? Where's her sense of adventure these days?" Venetia ranted on.

"Yes. What is there to do…" secretly chuckled Ruby. Her mother's ability to assume the worst about people or places was both puzzling and annoying.

Ruby knew that Sophie lived in London at Camden Town. She Googled the area to see what was there. That's when she learnt that there was a vocal course at At the Round. It had her name on it.

Venetia was lost for words once Ruby broke the news; slightly recovered, after considering Ruby's reasoning, she gave her approval at last: "I will have to call and see if Sophie will let you stay with her. I guess you're making good use of your break!"

"Thanks, Mum!" Ruby hugged her with such affection.

***

Packed lightly, Ruby travelled all by herself. First she had to take a train, which was easy. The railway in Britain is known for its friendly and helpful conductors. There were certainly advantages to listening to parents. She suddenly felt like she had a purpose in life. It felt good to be busy, determined, and feeling grown up. She sailed through the whole journey without any problems. Aunt Sophie, as her mother insisted Ruby called her, was already waiting in much anticipation at Victoria Station by the Nero Cafe, as agreed. Venetia pulled the latest pictures of Sophie straight off

Facebook. It would be hard to miss her bright colors, making her equal in bold fashion only to an African woman. The bright pink handbag and hat would have caught Ruby's attention anyway. Sophie looked classy, Ruby formed a solid opinion about her.

"Darling, look at you! You remind me of your mother so much!" She wasn't sure either it was a huge compliment or sheer disapproval. She had a vague idea what her mother really liked as a teen.

"Really? But I hope I've inherited dad's character then." They both laughed knowingly. Ruby was sure there was a high school history behind her mum and her friend.

"By the way, I insist, call me just Sophie please."

"Any plans for today?! I think we shall have a take away for dinner, if you don't mind? There is a fabulous Indian not too far." Sophie chatted away faster than the train Ruby just got off. It suited her fine though. She preferred to listen, even though she wasn't shy herself. Sophie had a completely different personality from her. It felt as though she needed to chat away, whereas Ruby didn't feel that way.

"How is your dear mother?"

"She's fine. She sends her warmest greetings. She says she'd love for you to come down for a visit."

"I must do. I must do. You'll see how busy London is. Perhaps I need to unwind. The trouble is once you put your roots down, especially in a place like this, it's hard to slow down. But everyone benefits from a good break once in a while. I hope you'll enjoy your stay. Shall we go and visit Camden Market today? The food hall there is to die for...."

"Sure. Sounds good!" Ruby was easy to please, interested in everything. Surprisingly, in spite of her slender figure, her mum's friend talked lots about food. It sounded odd. Undecided on her opinion of Sophie, Ruby decided to enjoy her company.

"Settled then. Let's catch a bus. You'll see a lot more this way."

Life in the mega city was always on the go. There were so many different nationalities everywhere: fused together by location and a common purpose of living, they got on with their lives happily. A song about it was already forming in her head.

"First of all, we'll drop your suitcase at home. Then we can walk to Camden."

"Ok."

Sophie was right. The bus idea was brilliant. Before Ruby knew it, they passed under a black iron gate, stepping into the Camden Market. Ruby was immediately pulled by the unique crafts and brightly displayed clothing. It was without doubt a trendy place. A young woman with light-lyric soprano was hitting high notes, blending them into a perfect melody, while someone else accompanied her on the guitar. Ruby hoped that after this week she would be a bit closer to singing just like that. Locking her eyes on the singer, she gave her a smile of approval.

Ruby could not wait to check all the stalls out. On the second level they had jewellery and paintings, odd and funniest sayings and more. She gasped in sheer awe. How could any one walk away without checking it all out? As she was reading quirky sayings, she felt someone staring at her.

"Ruby?" A familiar voice that reached straight to her heart called out her name.

"Alice?" Turning around, Ruby whispered back. She could hardly believe her eyes. Who was this elegant, much familiar stranger? It couldn't be her estranged older sister, surely not?!

"What are you doing here? How are you?" Alice fired the questions at her. Ruby could not get enough looking at her sister, a proper adult. Her deep green gypsy skirt and white blouse with intricate embroidery were eye catching. Ruby locked her gaze on her sister's face, realizing just how much she had longed for such an encounter.

"I'm staying with Mum's friend Sophie for a week. She's just getting lunch" Ruby feeling suddenly nervous, chatted away. "You disappeared without even a word! What exactly happened?"

"I'm surprised the parents didn't fill you in." Alice looked away, somewhere in the distance for a moment, being thoughtful.

"No. They never seem to talk about you. Sorry, this must sound awful."

"I'm really sorry too. I've missed you the most. Often I attempted to write, but stopped, lost for the right words to say. Mum and I had a falling out. She didn't see me as an adult who is able to make decisions of her own. Both of them didn't approve of my boyfriend. He's history now."

"Why didn't you say anything? Why didn't you return home?

"Not sure. Once you taste London life, it pulls you in. But for me it was more the main issue. I wished to prove I was an adult." Alice paused, looking at Ruby who was catching her every word. Then she added: "I'm still very angry with mother." Alice being honest, let her bottled up hurt out.

"Now that I found you, I'd love to see more of you! Here is my mobile number," Ruby was pleading.

"Sounds lovely. Take care. I'm here on business. I'll call you tonight." Alice explained with much affection in her voice.

"Look forward to it," Ruby said in a daze. She couldn't believe that she had just spoken with her big sister. They embraced each other, holding on for a while in the middle of a busy market. Everything seemed just a boring background. Then Alice rushed off to her meeting.

"Ruby! Over here. I got us an Ethiopian dish. Isn't this wonderful, not leaving the city we are tasting the flavours of the world!" Sophie was finally returning with food. Ruby realized how precious every moment was, so much can happen in the few moments it takes to get some lunch.

"This does look healthy!" Landing in London was turning out to be quite an adventure. The food of different colours was piled up on a spongy looking pancake. Then she took a bite. The taste was unusually delicious, slightly sour. Chewing slowly, Ruby was miles away now. She couldn't wait to see Alice again soon.

"Do you like it? This is injera, a traditional sour pancake made out of teff flour. I adore Ethiopian food."

"It's different!" Ruby approved, savouring the taste.

"Have you had enough of this place?"

"I think so." Her head was spinning from all the excitement around. The tourists were everywhere. Another gifted musician singing and strumming on the guitar at the café drew Ruby as a magnet. Two bags of purchases were secured on her shoulder. She was pleased with her bargains:

Doc Martin shoes half the price; a chunky knitted sweater; a multi-coloured scarf and two pairs of dangling earrings. One pair for her sister, she had decided. What a miracle to run into her like this! As she and Sophie sat at the café for a much needed break, listening to the soul-touching songs, suddenly it hit her. If she sat at home, feeling sorry for herself, she would have missed this opportunity. She felt rather sorry for being moody with James. God planned it all along. Yet all she could see when James had told her he was going away, was that he was dumping her. What a fool that I have been! And how could her parents let Alice go? Ruby just sat there, shaking her head.

"Is everything alright, darling?" Sophie questioned.

"Everything is awesome!" Ruby gave her a radiant smile.

"Everything can't be better!" Ruby had a new tone in her voice.

Later, back at the flat, Ruby asked whether Sophie knew of a church in the neighbourhood. The vocal course was not till Monday morning.

"No idea, darling, as I'm not a religious person. But I can list all the theatres there are for you."

"Thank you. Not sure if my mum had mentioned to you. I'm a Christian now. I would like to go to church this Sunday. I can look it up on the Internet."

"As you wish." Sophie raised her eyebrows. "Feel free to use the computer."

It took a few clicks to find information about local churches. She was spoiled for choice in the city. Ruby chose an evangelical church which had a clear, biblical statement of faith. She remembered Greg saying that it was most important before you join a church. It started at 10:30 am. Prayerfully Ruby sent a text, inviting Alice to meet up just outside the building. The reply didn't wait long: "Would love to. See u tomorrow. Love, Alice."

After tea and yet another take away, Sophie was relaxing with the newspaper and an herbal tea by the fire.

"I'm really curious. What was my mother like when you were teens?" Ruby fired out of the blue.

"I was wondering if you would be curious about our youth rebellion!"

"The thing is that Mum works a lot and when she comes home, she is exhausted from all the talking and organizing parties. She makes sure everyone else is pleased and happy."

"Life does that to you. We had fun back then." Sophie's voice was full of wistfulness.

"Can you please share what you were into? Please, Aunt Sophie?"

"Ok, since I'm aunt now." Sophie gave her a broad smile. "Let me think. What first comes to mind…There was this teacher who asked both your mum and I for our homework every single lesson. She clearly had supernatural energy reserves. Or so we thought at the time. On the very last day of school, we crushed two sleeping pills and added them to her tea. She fell asleep at the precise moment when the head master was doing his rounds wishing everyone a good summer."

"Did you get in trouble for that?"

"Oh, yes. We could have been expelled from school in those days," Sophie affirmed.

"So, what happened after?" pressed Ruby.

"We had to read with the reception kids for a term. That was a good cure!"

"That's all? Not much of a punishment if you ask me!"

"Only because the boys outdid us! The head master was busy dealing with them."

Sophie took a sip of her herbal tea. Then she continued digging up the past. "On that last day we had the whole school assembly. A few of the boys that we were good friends with made a bet." Sophie carefully placed her china cup on the table, building momentum. "The bet was to climb up on the roof of the school. When everyone was about to leave, start throwing boxes of tomatoes and eggs down."

"Did they dare do it?" Ruby almost couldn't believe that someone would keep such a dare!

"It was like a crazy rain coming down," Sophie assured here.

"No!" Ruby gasped, placing her hand over her mouth.

"That was an unthinkable thing to do. Very progressive behaviour for the late '70s, considering they used to punish us regularly with the rod. No matter what you do, the rebellion in us will surface sooner or later."

"Interesting." Ruby was ready to strike while the iron was hot. "This is precisely what the Bible teaches. There is no one good, not even one without God. We constantly rebel against His rules!"

"Hmmmm, if you put it that way... As a psychologist I can agree with the Bible on that."

Ruby smiled from delight. What an unexpected turn in their conversation.

"We better rest. Enough tales for one day."

"Sure thing. Good night!" Ruby felt so light-hearted as she climbed the stairs. Sophie put down the fire.

"Good night, sweetheart. Sleep well".

The grey stone church building was enormous. Ruby was wondering what year it had been built. Probably Victorian. A big banner, stretched outside, welcomed everyone to attend the services. People of different nationalities were passing up and down the street while Ruby waited for her sister.

"Hi, there!" Alice tapped her on the shoulder. She looked so pretty. Tall and blond, the complete opposite of Ruby, she would have looked good in anything. Today she had a denim jacket over a flowery dress with brown boots and brown leather belt. Ruby liked these accessories very much.

"Oh, I didn't see you. So many interesting people pass here. I got a bit dizzy from looking around."

"This is London for you. What's up with the church? I was hoping we could meet at the coffee house."

"It would be a yes on any other day. On Sunday I go to church. Shall we go?"

Alice was taken by surprise, but followed her none the less.

"A warm welcome to you, ladies!" An elderly Jamaican man greeted them with his grin.

"Hello!" Ruby stretched her hand out. They took an order of service from him and slid into the last pew.

The teaching of the Bible was very similar to the church in Newquay. Ruby was amazed how similar believers were. Except here no one wore flip flops, but were dressed rather smart. Her sister was concentrating hard to make sense out of Ruby's new found faith. After the service, coffee was offered and they stayed to chat.

"So, how's your life?" Ruby wished to know everything.

"Remember my boyfriend? I was really sweet on him. Mother didn't approve, saying that I'm wasting my life. Not working hard enough in school and blah blah blah. Dad took her side when I expected him to understand and support me. So I moved in with my boyfriend."

"What happened then?"

"We had our play at happy family. But we were very different people. I think he was resentful of me succeeding in life. It broke my heart. I'm making my own way in life. No need for any man." Alice spilled her resentment out.

"What did you do after you arrived here?"

"I enrolled on a university course in nutrition. Enjoyed it and made the most of it. I work for Waitrose."

"Wow! I don't understand why mum and dad never talked about what happened. Are you angry at them?"

"Yes and no. Certainly not with you. I'm grateful that I had to grow up and make my own decisions in life. I appreciate the freedom that I have. But I can never forgive mum and dad for not standing by me when I needed them the most. They were right about my boyfriend. That's true, but they should have let me make my own mistakes. And when I stumbled, they should have picked me up and loved me. That's what I'd do anyway if I ever have kids."

"Only Jesus loves unconditionally. Our parents could never do it without God's help." Ruby shared her bit of knowledge. "Mum is improving I think. How I wish that you phoned though."

"Please, don't be cross with me, Ruby. Anger and hatred have a very strong power over you at times. I was living in an emotional fog. I didn't want to be in touch with the mum and dad. I didn't want to get you in any trouble by being in touch."

"Anything would be better than silence." Ruby insisted, feeling betrayed.

"What are your plans while in London?" Alice asked, changing the subject.

"I'm on a vocal course here. It is a week long. I hope we can see each other as often as we can."

"Of course."

"I'll pray you will make up with mum and dad."

"That's impossible. Not a chance."

"God is in the business of miracles."

"Let's wait and see. If I were you, I would not get my hopes up."

"There is a verse in the Bible that explains what faith is. Let me find it for you." It took Ruby a few minutes, but at last she found it. "Here it is: 'Faith is the assurance of things hoped for, the conviction of things not seen.' Basically, God requires it of me. I must believe when I pray."

"Ok. If that works for you."

"It does."

"When are we meeting again?" Ruby was catching up on what she missed out.

"Tomorrow."

"Great. Look, they have a midweek Bible study." Ruby was on a mission. "Shall we go?"

"If you like. I want to spend as much time as I can together, my darling sister."

"Ok, see you tomorrow."

Giving her sister a warm embrace as a farewell, Ruby stood still watching her walk away. Meeting her again like that was the best present from the Lord. Ruby knew that even her beautiful, kind and multitalented sister needed God's help just the same.

16

James waved one more time to his mum as he followed Greg towards the boarding passage. The stewardess welcomed them. The big comfortable chairs were a treat in business class. Refreshments seemed to be flowing every few minutes. Overwhelmed, James savoured every moment.

"This is the life. How can I ever go back to economy after this?"

Greg shook his head, laughing. "It's more private here. Business people can go over their plans, so they can work undistractedly. In fact, we must have a Basic Briefing Meet to go over our working schedule."

"Now I feel like I'm one of you!" James's excitement was spilling out.

"Your responsibility will be to focus on interpreting mainly. Also, observe and learn what you can. Be professional at all times. Rely on God's strength at all times. You will have to wear a Coolmax bulletproof vest under your clothes once we are operational. Is everything clear?"

"Yes. I'll do my very best to match those requirements. And I've downloaded my Spanish app."

"Excellent. We'll worry about everything else," David confirmed.

David and Greg continued their discussion of the mission in hushed voices.

James put his headphones on, relaxing. He had to be in top shape not to let anyone down. The feeling as though he was walking on the water, like Peter in the Bible, was thrilling. He wondered why Peter started to drown after only a few steps when Jesus himself was right there. He sure hoped he would not drown while interpreting.

Xoxocotlan Airport in Oaxaca was packed with colour: sombreros, ponchos, dresses, bags – everything seemed to be screaming with the abundance of the land and culture, giving an instant flavour of Mexico.

The minute they stepped outside, stretching their legs, a heat wave hit them hard.

"How can locals survive in this sauna?" Greg bawled.

"It'll take time to get used to it," David pointed out.

James had his first opportunity to use his knowledge of Spanish. David asked him to order a cab.

Greg looked at David surprised. "What's wrong with the GetTaxi app?"

"Nothing. James needs to build up his confidence."

James took a deep breath and went to the stand advertising cab services. He was holding on to the piece of paper with the address of the B&B on it as if his life depended on it.

"Necesitamos un taxi para tres, por favour," James finally managed to say.

The Mexican with the wide grin nodded, answering back in perfect English. "Of course, sir."

"Thank you very much." James cheered up. "Perhaps it will not be half bad."

"Looks like he understands you," Greg encouraged him.

The cab man rushed towards them, taking most of the luggage with his bare hands and asked them to follow him.

The drive to the B&B didn't take long. Looking out of the window, James enjoyed the scenery. The palm trees and terracotta roofs were everywhere. Life wasn't in a rush here. People seemed warm and welcoming. James was in love with this place already.

While David and Greg were both talking on their phones to the local drug dealing unit that was expecting them, James went to the bar and ordered himself a massive glass of ice cold hibiscus flower cordial. It just hit the spot.

"We're going to grab something to eat and be off!" David instructed them.

"The men from the Mexican Intelligence Agency are expecting us. A few of them speak decent English. I think your job just got easier," David teased.

At the agency Sr. Fernandez introduced everyone to his team of men. James kept his back super straight whilst shaking hands with short, but exceptionally strong men.

"BBM is in ten minutes," was the announcement. James nodded knowingly, familiar with the terminology now.

The plan was to travel to the cannabis growing places, have negotiations with the local farmers and try to educate them what this drug is doing to the young people. Greg prepared the figures and the information on the latest research findings. James could not believe it all. After Greg informed them that several independent studies confirmed the same effect of marijuana on teens, he never wanted to go near the stuff. Schizophrenia? Paranoia? No, thank you. The importance of what they were doing kicked in once again.

"The travelling will begin tomorrow. We have to leave at 5 am before the heat of the day. Then we'll have a good break as everything is normally shut at noon. Then we'll continue to travel through the evening, depending on the outcome of the first negotiations."

"Are you ready?" Greg wondered.

"For our mission? Can't wait."

"Dinner, first. Let's eat on the roof." James climbed the stairs at top speed.

The view from the roof was magnificent. The flower pots were everywhere, full of bright colours. Green cactuses sat proudly, as though guardians of the place. The fire pit was lit, some torches gave a flickering, warm light. James could see the peak of the mountains rising in the distance. The atmosphere was captivating. The heat of the day finally subsided. James's stomach was growling as he smelled the food.

"Let's tuck in. Lord, please bless this food and our time here. Amen." David encouraged them.

James took a bite of the purple corn tortilla with baked vegetables. The taste was gentle and sweet. He had never tried anything tastier. The rest of the dishes were just as phenomenal.

"Isn't it amazing that God gave us so much to eat and to enjoy, yet we are craving something else that harms us. Did you know, while I was collecting info on the effect of drugs, I came across the results of two separate studies. That was special research how cannabis affects teens. Turns out that when it is regularly used, besides psychiatric disorders, its usage destroys the feel good chemical in the brain. This particular chemical inspires us to be excited about life. How about that?"

"Satan offers his counterfeit, instead of what God installed in us free to enjoy, making people dependant. There is always a price to pay," James elaborated.

"True. When we reject God's gifts, we are rejecting life itself," Greg concluded.

"It's getting late. We have an early start tomorrow. Has everyone had enough?"

"The best food ever!" was all James could say, his hunger pangs fully satisfied. They all broke into a vigorous laughter.

The early morning in Oaxaca was breath-taking. The sky was painted with colours: light blue slowly turning into pale purple. After a rushed breakfast, everyone was loaded into the van. They were ready to go.

James still was not hungry after last night's feast. The feeling of anticipation was rising instead. He was in the same country as his father, just thinking about it gave him jelly legs.

Two hours later after a roller coaster road that was full of spectacular landscapes with waterfalls, lush vegetation, and unsuspecting goats chewing contentedly by the side of the road, they finally arrived at the mountain village.

"Locals are very superstitious about this place. Apparently one of the saints appeared here many moons ago, warning them of the evil spirits. The legend didn't help farmers. Not many businessmen want to trade here. They prefer to go elsewhere to buy corn, agave, bananas and coffee," the agent shared.

"Miguel! Miguel!" Agent Rodrigues shouted.

"Si. Coming." The reply came through the door. A sturdy, medium height man with a thick black moustache walked out.

"We need to talk," the Mexican agent announced. "Get all the men together. We're meeting at 10 a.m. in Santa Maria village square. Tell everyone this is a matter of urgency! It's an order for everyone to be there." James was all ears. He could catch the general meaning, but not every word. Hopefully by the end of the trip he would be fluent.

Next morning the village square was full of farmers and their families. There was one white man, definitely not a farmer, who stood out of place with a young, pleasant-looking lady was by his side. She towered straight, with confidence and calmness about her. James could tell that he wasn't the only one who spotted them. Greg kept looking in their direction, distracted. James grinned noticing his interest.

"Hola," the agent greeted everyone.

"Today we have brought important guests with us. They flew in from UK. The operation is a collaborative work of our and their countries. They brought orders that will concern all of you. They work for the drug apprehension unit. Please listen carefully."

"Hello! Buenos Dias! My name is David. Greetings to you all. We are blessed to visit Mexico. The unparalleled beauty and abundance of your land is impressive." The loud cheer and clapping interrupted his speech. David looked surprised, not used to expressions of such emotions. James had his own battle to fight. Feeling as though someone plunged him into an electric socket, his nerves were on fire. He had to think fast, as never before. Giving James a few minutes to interpret, David continued unfazed. "However the reason why we had to come isn't a pleasant one. We apprehended a drug dealer back in England. His trail of supply led us here, to Oaxaca." The faces around began to look troubled.

"The truth is that the latest research reveals that the frontal cortex is much more affected by drugs during adolescence. This is a big problem because many drug dealers use young people to deliver and take drugs."

James suddenly went blank. He looked at David. "I don't think I can translate that. Too complex."

David stopped talking, thrown off his track once again. He helplessly looked around. At that moment a white man stood up. "I'm the local doctor. This young man is doing a splendid job. Perhaps I can translate this rather complex matter."

David gratefully nodded, approving. "Much appreciated." With much ease the doctor conveyed the message in Spanish.

David continued, "We have an offer for you. You have to turn your fields into growing something else, whatever you choose. The cannabis has to go. If you do not comply with our terms, the army men will be hired to come and burn if all off. This has to happen."

Suddenly chaos broke out, everyone shouting at once.

"What's going on?" Both David and Greg helplessly turned to the doctor for explanation.

"They are very unhappy. The superstition has a strong hold on them here."

"Silencio, por favor! Quiet everyone!" The agent shouted out.

The hush fell instantly.

"Go home, hombres! Think about it long and hard. The evil must be stopped. You have no choice in this matter." David's voice sounded as hard as metal. The farmers reluctantly got up. One after another they began to leave the square. The doctor approached the men.

"Hello, amigo!"

"Good to see you Dr. Davidson. How are you? And Sabine?" The Mexican agent inquired.

"Can't complain. Will you please introduce me to your British friends?" The doctor was determined.

"It will be my pleasure."

"Hello, I'm Dr. Davidson, a doctor and a missionary. My daughter Sabine and I have been here for many years." Sabine was happily chatting with the local kids.

David shook hands with him gladly.

"Amazing. Your commitment to this community is impressive. Can't be easy."

"You're right about that. Superstition is the biggest enemy I have to fight. I love this country and especially the people here. They are open, sincere, and friendly. We have been made very welcome here."

"I would be honoured if you stopped by for some coffee at my house," he continued while the attention of the men was on him. "I know you must be extremely busy, but my proposition could be of use to you in this situation. I've been praying for a long while about this drug growing business. I might have a solution."

"Please, lead the way. We have to wait for the farmers to come around. It could take a while. With your knowledge and expertise with the locals, you can help us no doubt."

"I'll lead the way." He quickly spoke to the Mexican agents, explaining that he had to borrow their guests for a while. David, Greg and James followed right after him. Sabine joined them as soon as her father waved to her. She was promptly introduced to the men. In spite of the heat of this place, she was very modestly dressed in a blue and yellow dress. She had a sense of intelligence about her , listening attentively to the conversation about the farmers and the mission of these men. At the house, painted in bright indigo, the kettle was already on.

"Sabine, can we please have some of your legendary coffee for our guests." The doctor kindly ordered his daughter. Average in height, this young lady was extraordinary. James guessed she was in her early twenties. She seemed kind and respectful, with a sharp mind. How could she not miss all the modern technology and comfort? Not to mention the anxiety of dealing with the ever-present creepy-crawlies that made their residence in that area. The insects here were ginormous. James was constantly on the lookout for the scorpions that were in abundance here. The size of them was unreal.

"Yes, papa, of course," she answered sweetly.

They seemed to be very close.

"The coffee comes from nearby Sierra. To die for," the doctor informed with pride.

Sitting comfortably in the living room, James looked around. The house was decorated so differently than anything he had seen before. Multi-coloured and stripy rags covered the floor. Skilfully made tapestries adorned the walls. Wooden furniture gave a feel of rural outdoors. The tropical flowers outside were thriving in their blues, pinks and yellows.

"I'm not going to beat around the bush. I've been looking into benefits of medical cannabis for cancer patients. The remedy is proved to be effective. I produced a small batch of oil that I use in my treatment. It brought astounding results. Turns out cannabidiol was a remedy valued by the Ancients. My hope is that the crops can be saved and used for medicinal purposes. Of course, it will not be easy at first. You need supply and demand. The biggest risk is drug dealers who will not give up easily. I won't be able to pull it off by myself."

"Certainly sounds interesting. We don't know enough about cannabis, I have to agree. I've read that an ancient tomb of 5000 years old had been discovered with the cannabis leaf in it. They surely valued it highly," David added.

"Definitely worth a try," Greg agreed. "We must convince the farmers not to be so easily scared of the drug dealers who will approach them again. When you don't fight evil, it will swallow you up."

Sabine nodded in agreement. "Your visit is an answer to our prayers."

"We're here on behalf of our government. However, we also serve the higher King just like yourselves." David acknowledged his faith.

"I was thinking why not pioneer a cancer treatment centre right here in the mountains. We'll find patients. This dreadful disease is on the rise. Hopefully with so many people coming and going, the drug dealers will be scared to interfere." Greg developed his thought further.

"If the farmers still get paid, that will be a decisive factor," the doctor confirmed. "Mexicans are generously sacrificial. They'll elevate the needs of others above their own if there's a way not to starve their own families. God can soften hearts once they hear about this project." The doctor knew the people well.

"Anyone with a conscience must be pleased that the same plants are being used for healing, not for destruction." Sabine gave her first speech with conviction while pouring the coffee into the cups. The smell was delicious.

"How very true!" Greg agreed. She gratefully smiled back.

"Why don't you lead us all in prayer? We'll heartily agree with you as we're all believers ourselves." David asked the doctor. He didn't need to be asked twice.

Dr. Davidson bowed his head and began to pray. His words were precise and to the point. You could tell he was a man who spent time in prayer. He sounded like he was comfortable in God's presence.

David, Greg, James and Sabine, united, sealed his prayer with a firm and loud "Amen."

"When are you heading back?" asked the doc.

"Not sure yet. As soon as we wrap up the business here. We have a B&B reserved in Oaxaca, but it is a very bumpy ride back to the hotel."

"True that," he laughed heartily. "These are not American roads, but it makes it all the more exciting. You're welcome to stay with me. I would be honoured."

"Thank you. How hospitable of you."

"Please excuse me. I better start looking for supporters in the States. We'll see what happens."

"Does anyone want to jump off the bridge into the local river? It's really pleasant in this heat," offered Sabine.

"Sure!" both James and Greg said in unison.

David noticed a spark between his colleague and Sabine.

"Go and play, kids. I'll stay behind, in case of any urgent business."

James could not remember when he had so much fun. The bridge was just the right height. The water cool and clear, refreshing in this hot weather like nothing else. James kept going again and again, while Sabine and Greg sat down talking.

"Watch my back flip," shouted James. Sabine and Greg applauded, impressed.

"I can do that!" Greg got up and began to climb the bridge.

"Common, old man," cheered on James

"Careful, young man. Experience is something that comes with age. Don't knock it!"

Sabine laughed, amused at their banter.

Greg's phone began to ring. "It's your phone. Shall I answer?" Sabine wondered.

"Yes, please. I'll be right there."

"It's David. He says we need to head back at once."

"Ok. Tell him we're on our way."

James could see a rapid friendship developing between Greg and Sabine.

Walking back was so pleasant after a short swim. Back at the house light refreshments were waiting for them.

"Had a good time? Guess what, there are a few friends who are willing to risk and provide financial backing for the healing clinic. Now we can speak to the farmers. A soul-touching message is a must though. Greg, are you up for the task?"

"Sure," Greg rose to the challenge once more.

"James, are you feeling confident?" David turned toward him.

"I can give it a go. It will be tricky though." He was honest about it.

"Perhaps I can be of help?" offered Sabine.

"You're on. Much appreciated."

***

In the evening, all the farmers returned looking grumpy. Curious, they still did not like being disturbed from their usual routine with the threat to their income looming over them. As the darkness of the evening fell, a disruptive atmosphere was brewing. They were about to start the meeting, when the doctor realized he didn't have his pager on.

"I'd better get my pager in case someone needs me urgently. Please start without me."

Greg whispered something in Sabine's ear. She nodded, then walked out. A few moments later she was back with an eight year old boy: tanned, with a white row of teeth, he looked as healthy as they come.

"Dear farmers! Back home the kids look exactly the same as this one. Perhaps not as tanned." A murmur like a breeze swept through the room. "They are the same as this lad as far as their interests, desires go. They love to play football, have a good time, ride their bikes and learn. All kids are the same around the world. But evil men come and change their childhood forever. They have an effective hook: drugs and deception. So, instead of enjoying life, the kids as young as this lad, are becoming involved in distribution and taking it. The drug dealers are very cunning. They don't care about anything but their own pockets. You can't continue to assist them in their evil. Now you have an opportunity to fight back. That's why we need your help. The power of doing good or evil is in your hands. Strong superstition lives among you. You have to let it go. God is the only One, who has the real power over our lives. We must listen only to God through the Bible, as Doctor Davidson has been teaching you all for years. The superstition is a powerfully deceptive, but God is still stronger. We are fighting an invisible war here." Convicting silence fell upon those listening.

"While you are digesting this information, I have a proposition for you. You can continue to grow marijuana and get paid just as much, but it will be used for medicinal purposes. Dr. Davidson is willing to pioneer a clinic here. What do you say? You would be able to help sick people instead of bringing on the sickness and destruction."

"What about the drug dealers? Who will take them on?" someone shouted out.

"You will have to stand strong and refuse to deal with them. Above all pray for God's protection."

Sabine put her whole heart into her words, having much love for these people.

"Good job interpreting." David was grateful. "Have you done anything like this before?"

Sabine beamed at him. "Yes, a few times I helped my father. I learned the language before he did. Now he does fine on his own." Her father still was nowhere to be seen.

Meanwhile, Doctor Davidson grabbed his pager, intending to head back to the meeting. Then he spotted a man, looking out of place, with his face painted in the Mayan style. He was lurking around, looking for something or someone.

"Can I help you?" the doctor offered.

The man startled, not expecting to hear a white man speak in his native tongue.

"I know that there is going to be a meeting in the village. I must get to it," the man let out in hoarse voice, looking out through the pine trees.

"You don't look like a farmer. It concerns the farmers mostly."

"Nor do you. I'm on a mission and it has to be accomplished tonight," the man cut off curtly.

The way the stranger was talking disturbed him. Nothing seemed right about this man. Discerning that he must not lead the man to that meeting at any cost, he gave his best shot at it.

"Looks like you have been travelling from afar. Would you like to come in and have a strong cup of coffee?

Then I could help you to find the place you need," the doctor had to find out more.

"Good idea! I can do with something stronger than coffee too. Do you have any tequila?"

"It would not be Mexico if I didn't," the doctor's honesty was a credit to him.

As asked, the doctor pulled out a jar of tequila. As a rule he kept it in the house mostly for medicinal purposes. The stranger took the jar and went straight for the worm, before the doctor could say anything else. The trouble was, the worm, saturated in the liquid, made him drunk fast. Relaxed, he blurted out, "I have been hired by the drug dealers to disrupt that meeting. Bring it down to nothing."

"Oh, this is of interest to me. Please tell me more about it," the doctor urged him.

"I'm a sixth generation shaman. I've got power to do whatever I want!" The drink really loosened his tongue.

"I've got access to power too. I worship the true and living God. Would you mind if I show you His power through prayer?"

"Go on," the shaman scoffed at the challenge. The doctor closed his eyes. He began to plead that the blood of Christ, shed on the cross for evildoing sinners, would cleanse him from the demonic activity at this moment in time. The shaman's face became pale. He slowly rose from his seat.

"I must go." He grabbed his bag and run, somewhat sobered up. Concerned, the doctor looked out.

He saw shaman running around like a mad dog, bitten by a scorpion. The foam was coming out of his mouth. The doctor ignoring his escape kept on praying with new zest that the power of God would stop the evil intended towards the farmers. As the man disappeared in the distance, the doctor felt drained of all energy, collapsing in his chair.

***

"That was brilliant work! God powerfully moved in their hearts, not an easy situation for them," David rejoiced after the farmers all left. "Shall we have supper? Sabine, I hope your father prepared something for us. Where was he tonight?" Everyone agreed it was odd, unless there had been an emergency. Walking together in the dark with a powerful torch, they chatted away.

James still could not believe that the farmers agreed with their plans. David and Greg would be staying behind to team up with the local police to help to fish out some of the local, hard core drug dealers. Now it was time for James to visit his dad. His excitement was even stronger than his appetite or maybe not. Just picturing tamales wrapped in banana leaves, blandas, black beans, chicken with mole sauce and local cheese made him hungry. If only he could try a worm from a tequila jar. That would establish his reputation as a hard core traveller forever. If not, at least he could say he ate chapulines, fried grasshopper with salt and pepper, a newly discovered delicacy.

17

The grey London sky hung heavy. The brick buildings squashed against each other. The perpetual noise of constantly moving transport and people, buzzing about like bees, made Ruby's head spin. She wasn't used to it and felt suffocated. The litter on the floor irritated the eye and was the last drop. On the outside, autumnal city appeared as a scraggly vagabond. Observing such a view, breathing fumes instead of sea air, Ruby already missed the carved white cliffs back home. However, today nothing, not even gloomy grey skies, could dampen her spirit. With a spring in her stride, she couldn't wait to step into At the Round.

The building was impossible to miss. Cutting through the car park, she spotted sophisticated elegance of a modern building soon enough. Ruby swung the door, heading towards the receptionist.

"Hello, I'm here for the vocal course."

"Hello! Glad you could make it. Let me take your details. I'll write you a badge and you'll be good to go. Your tutor is already waiting for the students in the Michael Jackson Room. It's downstairs."

"Ok. That sounds promising," Ruby beamed at the lady.

"You'll be surprised what you'll be able to do before next Saturday," the receptionist knowingly informed.

"Look forward to it!" excitement poured out of her.

The Michael Jackson Room was full of teens who were chatting animatedly when she entered.

"Listen up, everyone! It's time to start. My name is Peter Anderson. I'm your humble servant and a tutor this week. There are a few musicians and singers who will be collaborating with you. They'll be introduced shortly. Now, who believes in true miracles?"

Ruby without even thinking raised her hand. She looked around, noticing that she was the only one. The rest of the students shyly were looking at each other unsure.

"One is always a start!"

"Excellent!" He nodded with encouragement in Ruby's direction. "By the end of this week all of you will compose your own music, write a song, sing a solo, play an instrument in a group with other musicians. And finally, the most exciting of all ... give a performance to family and friends. It might be a challenge, but it will happen. You'll become the biggest miracle yourself. Are you ready?"

"Yes!" A loud cheer filled the room.

"Ok. This is better. Let's go for it. What are we waiting for? I'll start by calling out your name. You'll have to tell me your music level, singing level, performance level. Anything that will help me to place you into the right group. Let's do it. Please take your seats."

Ruby grabbed the first chair. A rather tall young man slid onto a seat next to her.

"Hope you don't mind. I'm Christian by the way."

"Hi. I'm Ruby," she eagerly shot back.

Everything seemed like the best dream. No school, no boring lessons. She would be doing what she absolutely loves for a whole week. Plus, everyone here also loves music as much as she does. She could not wait for the end result of their labour.

The tutor separated them into groups, giving specific tasks. Some would have to learn a new melody to play, others had to sing it.

Christian the pianist, Ruby the singer and Leah the guitarist ended up in one group. The tutor gave them a piece of music to play and song to learn, to see how the three of them could work together.

Before Ruby realized, it was break time. Leah ran to meet up with her friends. Christian still was lingering around.

"Do you want a hot drink?" he faced Ruby casually.

"Sounds good." They headed towards the café.

"So, how did you hear about this course?" She was curious.

"I have an app. When they advertise a course, I get notifications about it. I've been playing piano forever. I felt like I was ready to take it to another level. I'd like to compose my own music."

"Really? That is very ambitious. I'm reading a book about Isaac Watts. Have you ever heard of him?"

"Not really."

"Joy to the world, the Lord is come! Let earth receive her King; Let every heart prepare Him room, and heaven and nature sing, and heaven and nature sing, and heaven and nature sing!" Ruby broke out into singing.

"Oh, yeah! I hear it all the time at the supermarkets during the winter holiday season. I never knew he wrote it."

"And many more. He was a writing machine, if you like. No one wrote more than him. He loved the Lord and felt that the music that glorifies God should be joyful, the very best."

"That sounds right," Christian agreed wholeheartedly.

"Do you believe in God?" he asked straight up.

"Yes, I do."

"What's your opinion on gay Christians?" he suddenly shot at her.

Ruby was taken aback. She didn't expect this. A verse from the Bible, that encouraged to be always ready to give an account of your faith, popped up. She filled her lungs with air as though ready for a dive, and let it out: "To be honest it doesn't really matter what I think, does it? All we care about must be what the Bible says about it? For example, lets use the songwriter, Isaac Watts. he can be of help to crack down this complex issue. Like any of us, he longed to be loved by another human being and be married at some point. However, rejected by the poetess that he fell in love with, he remained single, living a life of total obedience to God. 'Delight yourself in the Lord and He will give you the desires of your heart.' This became his reality and aim in life. I can imagine it wasn't easy or unfair as some might say, So, it was enough hard, but with God's strength, is achievable."

"So what does this mean for someone who is gay?"

"The Bible is clear that God has created male and female for companionship and procreation. Otherwise we are saying that God's way is wrong and our way is right, yeah? We don't try and challenge the law of gravity by jumping off tall buildings and expecting it to change.

Spiderman being an exception of course." Christian chuckled at her wit.

"Why would there be anything different about our sexuality?" she continued enthusiastically. "Our faith can't be based on feelings, but anchored in worship and adoration of God. I haven't been reading the Bible for long. I know that the book of Romans teaches that our sexuality is linked to who we worship in life." Ruby was on a roll now.

"Have you ever read about love of same sex couples being admired and encouraged through the history of mankind?" Ruby threw out a challenge.

Christian kept quiet for a while. Then, facing Ruby, with a frank look on his face, he admitted: "You do have a point. I see it now. But not everything is as simple though. What do you say about so-called Christian Britain persecuting gays in the 50s? Even Alan Turing, a code breaker during the war, who worked for Bletchley Park was forced to a treatment that must cure him from homosexuality."

"That was insane, I agree. Jesus never called His followers to persecute anyone, be it gays or people of other faiths. Jesus Christ is exclusive enough, claiming to be the only way to God. If this offends anyone, it is not God's fault, but our own. How can anyone complain about what God wants to do? Jesus calls to love, pray and warn about His coming. We must be delivered from our sinful, destructive ways and only He can do it. Everyone needs to know that." Ruby paused, thought about something and added: "The trouble is we, even as believers, get carried away. We love playing god at times."

"When you put it this way, I understand. I've read the book of Romans before. In spite of it making sense to you, it's contrary to what I feel and desire so it's impossible to do."

"You're right. Without God's help it will never be possible. We need the Holy Spirit to give us a hand." Ruby insisted firmly on it.

"Would you oppose gay marriage then?" Christian was determined to get this answers today.

"Yes, I do because God does. He knows best. This only seems complex, but it's simple when you think about it. Imagine, this is all we have to do: place God in the centre of our lives. And this is a tough call. Being caught up in time, we think differently to timeless eternity and what matters up there. Only God can harness our deceitful, but surely pleasant for a while feelings," She concluded with much passion.

"But in the meantime we make music, right?" Christian winked at Ruby, teasing her.

"That's right. Who is this gay person then?"

"I am. Can you still be friends?"

"Of course. I need help to walk in obedience as much as anyone, admitting that to God is what makes a Christian. Those who believe become closer than blood relatives," Ruby added heartily.

"I could do with some family! Acceptance or understanding doesn't come naturally to my parents," he pointed flatly.

"I'll pray for you." Ruby realized that she had been promising to pray a lot lately. It felt like a big task now, hopefully she was up to that.

"Thanks. Look, it is time to head back."

"Let's go." Ruby sped for the door at once. And she had thought she would only be practicing her vocals this week!

"I have a feeling we're not done talking on this topic, are we?" Christian chuckled.

"Not at all." Ruby gave him a wicked grin.

"Hey, would you like to come to a Bible study with me and my sister on Wednesday?"

"Sure. I'm in."

Ruby had never felt more alive because of this spiritual connection.

Life in London happened with great speed. Every day the vocal course At the Round flooded Ruby with newly acquired knowledge and new vocal skills. She got to sing solo with multiple instruments, her confidence was boosted no end. They were told to invite families for Saturday performance at 2 pm. This was nerve racking, considering that she would love to see both her parents and her sister there.

Ruby and Alice met every day, catching up on years of absence.

On Wednesday evening Ruby, Alice and Christian were meeting outside of the evangelical church in Camden.

"Have you been waiting long?" Alice greeted her warmly.

"Not that long. By the way this is my new friend, Christian." Ruby's voice rung with excitement.

Her sister affectionately shook his hand. "Pleased to meet you."

"Shall we go?" Ruby hurried them in. The three of them walked together. Ruby felt as though an unseen power was guiding her. They could go to so many places in the city, but in her heart she knew that they needed to be here tonight.

The midweek Bible study was from the Book of Genesis, chapter 34. It was a fascinating tale Ruby had never heard before. A man called Jacob had a family: two wives, twelve sons and only one daughter, Dinah. Even though Ruby had no brothers, whilst listening, she could identify herself with Dinah in many ways. This ancient story that happened centuries ago made perfect sense in her present circumstances. How was this even possible? Saying goodbye to the pastor, they headed towards a coffee shop. Ruby prayed and hoped that Saturday would be not only the end of her course, but mostly the end of hurt feelings in her family.

"What did you all think of the Bible story?" Ruby was curious as they made themselves comfortable in the armchairs.

"It was nothing like I expected. To be honest I've assumed that the Bible was an ancient book. Must be valuable. I saw it being displayed in the British Museum once. Personally, it had no effect on my life whatsoever. In church, when the preacher was explaining the story from this ancient book, I felt like it just happened, like something you would hear on the news. It made so much sense to me suddenly. Jacob's dysfunctional family is so relatable." Alice added quietly: "Every family is a bit like that."

"I agree. I've learned much myself. Even God's chosen people weren't always perfect. A youth can relate to Dinah's mistake, being bored and adventurous at the same time. Don't you agree?" Christian looked to the sisters for approval.

"Yeah. Especially, we can relate to the disaster that her brothers made out of it." Ruby teased him.

"Good not to have any, right? We would be in a bigger mess." Alice joined in. The three of them laughed so loud it caught the attention of everyone in the café. Ruby mouthing "sorry" across the room made an apology.

"What was encouraging was that God overruled such terrible behaviour. Israel still received twelve tribes that these brothers made up!"

"That is one powerful story." Christian sealed his freshly formed opinion.

"Perhaps He can help our family after all?" Ruby reasoned, facing Alice.

"It did remind of my falling out with my parents," Alice joined in. A flashback became powerfully vivid. Alice loved growing up by the sea. Only this time, she had caught a wave and was riding it high on her body board. Suddenly the feeling of utter helplessness, when the weight of the disagreement came crashed over her head like a huge wave, hit her. It was impossible to catch a breath of air. A lot of energy was needed to regain the balance, to keep on going. Once she fell out with her parents, she was all at sea, with no board, unable to carry on bodysurfing, destined aimlessly swim for her life.

"I was so selfishly stubborn at the time. I can see now how all of us were at fault," she arrested both Ruby and Christian's attention. "The preacher was saying that the Bible doesn't encourage sex before marriage. I thought two people need to know each other before they commit. Such a mistake is conveniently alluring, but nonetheless deceptive. We were together, but going in different ways: I wished for a career, he resented that. The hurt of breaking up after knowing each other intimately is unbearable," explained Alice frankly.

"I've discovered that when I have no one to cry out to, God is always there, listening. I have a friend who is really good on a paddle board. Even in the wind, he manages to keep his balance. Jesus is the one who can pull us right back onto the board, restoring the balance, giving the strength to conquer the biggest waves. I don't have to make a lot of mistakes first. In fact God wishes to do everything and anything to stop that." Ruby poured her heart out.

"What's the biggest wave you wish you could surf?" Christian threw out a challenge.

"With God's help I can surf 40 feet!" Ruby got fired up. "And I only done body surfing before!"

"I love your attitude!" Alice encouraged her heartily, beaming back at her.

"But what do you estimate is a spiritual equivalent to surfing that monster wave?" Ruby challenged them back.

"Thinking of Dinah, probably forgiving her family after they brought her back home after killing her newlywed." Alice spoke with such perception as though she had been there and done that herself.

"Interesting you say that because this summer I visited a church for the first time. It was called Surfer's Church," Ruby revealed. "On the walls surf boards had the names of Dinah's brothers who became twelve tribes of Israel. I was just connecting the dots of the story for myself. There must have been true forgiveness and reconciliation on both sides in the family. In God's eyes only those who desire to imitate His Son Jesus have His favour and back up in life. And He powerfully blessed them by turning one family into a nation! Dinah was the reason her brothers went to the city of men who didn't worship true and living God. But they did all the killing. It was not a light thing to get over and to make up with her and with God again."

Sensing Alice's openness, Ruby seized her opportunity to translate the moral of the story into their personal issue. "By the way, Mum and Dad are coming on Saturday for my performance. Would you like to come too?"

"Thank you for inviting me. I have a lot to think through first."

"Of course. Take your time." Ruby encouraged her, hoping for a real turn around.

"Isn't it forgiveness that makes the world go around?!" Christian whispered under his breath.

All of a sudden Alice seemed eager to leave. "It's getting late. We better head home."

"Ok." Ruby felt the depth and weight of this conversation herself, like a concentrated cordial that scorches the throat. They all needed to think.

Walking out, they still chatted, making plans when to meet again. Alice was sold out that Ruby must visit Prince Albert and Victoria Museum and attend a play at the Globe.

"You have to see all what the city has to offer," she kissed her tenderly. They both smiled knowingly, having a closer bond that was growing speedily.

"What a real pleasure to meet you, Christian. See you around." It was time to go separate ways for now.

18

James looked at the phone. He had not heard from Ruby at all. But there was a long text from his mum. She told him about her tennis lessons again and copied a short extract from her friend, Maggie, who was blogging now. "James, darling, have a read. This is good. Love u and miss u, Mum. "

The blog entry followed: "How to deal with sin radically. I have been a keen gardener all my life. There are multiple weeds that come up in my garden. You name it: deadnettle, brambles, celandine or cat's ear. Alexanders, for example, have multiple roots that grow everywhere. No matter what I do, it comes up persistently every year. The only way to keep it under control is to pull it with the root. If I don't do anything about it, it spreads like wild fire. Only after I've worked hard to clear it can I plant lavender or any other flowers, making the garden attractive for the butterflies or bees. In the middle of summer the bees buzz right in, sucking on the nectar. The spiritual moral is this: the Lord wants us to keep our hearts, free from weeds, but full of delicious aroma from the blossoms. It will NOT happen by itself. If there is a particular sin that the Lord is convicting you of, uproot it once and for all. Pray fervently against it, don't be purely convicted about it!!! Keep pulling the roots out. It will have no choice, but to go."

James could just envision Maggie's garden back in Brighton, full of English lavender and bees. It looked so restful up there. He got the point. He bowed his head and prayed right there and then. James said sorry for being afraid and selfish, accepted the forgiveness promised, asking the Lord to help him to be more like Him.

***

Back in London, Ruby was rushing to the café to grab something to eat when she heard someone catching up with her.

233

"Hey, you!"

"Hey, Christian! How's it going?"

"Brilliant. I think I have my first song. Could not sleep last night, so it just came to me. Do you want to hear it?"

"Of course! Bring it on!"

"Shall we find a piano somewhere after we're finished today?"

"Great. Look forward to it."

To find a room with a piano didn't prove to be difficult. Before Ruby knew it, Christian broke into his new song. The reggae rhythm filled the air. Ruby instantly enjoyed the funky beat. He sang about people who are rushing about their business in a big city. But what is the point to our existence? Everything will pass – beauty, jobs, fame, money - then what is the point of living? The song picked Ruby's soul up, carrying it above the ground, taking her up, past the tallest building in the city, giving her a bird's eye view. And then the chorus came in. "Lift up your eyes to the cross. Trust Jesus and thrive. Crucified, yet alive, He is patiently waiting to embrace you."

"It's amazing. I don't even know what to say..."

"You're the one who told me that Watts wanted to write cheerful Christian music. Here you have my attempt. Will you sing it with me for Saturday's performance please?"

"It will be a privilege. I'd love to." Ruby was taken aback by the offer, yet super excited.

"It's a 'yes' then?"

"Yes, of course! Let's go and see what our tutor says about it?"

"Let's hope he will be on board."

Ruby gave Christian a friendly hug, bursting with such pride for him. "You are a raw talent. I just hope and pray my family will turn up as well as my sister. This could go either way, but I'm asking for a miracle! Are your folks coming?"

"Not sure." Christian didn't feel like talking about it and Ruby didn't want to pry.

On Saturday morning the buzz of mixed feelings was in the air: the day of the final performance. As far as Ruby knew everyone was coming. She spent much time in prayer that God would soften her parents' hearts. She wished Alice was back in her life permanently.

The room was ready, all the equipment plugged in and sound checked. Last sound checks. The room was semi dimmed. Ruby will break the news to her parents after the concert was over. She decided it was a wise option.

Ruby and Christian's turn came at last. Ruby took the centre stage looking radiant. As Christian began gently, but confidently pressing piano keys, Ruby's voice lifted to the ceiling, travelling around the room. She sang with newly acquired skill, putting all her strength into it, as though it was her first and last performance. At the end of her rendering of the song, the audience erupted with a loud cheer. Someone shouted:" Bravo! Go, kids!" Others joined in, turning their praise into a standing ovation. Ruby bowed once more, then started making her way towards her parents. The next student was already up.

"Darling, it was just phenomenal," her dad embraced her affectionately.

"I had no idea you were so talented. And that young man who played as well!" Sophie exclaimed.

"So proud of you!" Her mother's excitement spilled over.

"The big surprise is yet to come. I hope you're all ready for it." Ruby turned around and waved. Alice began to make her way toward her family.

Venetia put her hand over her mouth, overcome with such an emotion.

"Mum! Dad!" was all Alice could say, beaming at them. Ruby could tell her sister had done some wrestling and put the past behind.

"Alice, darling! Look at you." Marcus opened his arms.

"You look well. Thank God for that," he gently whispered. Venetia rushed over, clasping them both. It was a powerful picture to remember, wishing she could frame the atmosphere of the moment forever, Ruby felt overjoyed.

Sophie stood there, watching, not sure what to do with herself. Only a blind person could miss the significance of the moment.

"Shall we all go for a drink? Ruby, make sure you invite your friend. It doesn't look like his folks are here today." Venetia sounded like herself again, wishing to have everything under control.

"Will do. Thanks, Mum."

"I have an even better idea. Why don't we hop on the tube and visit the Victoria and Prince Albert Museum? Ruby will enjoy it immensely," proposed Alice.

"What a brilliant idea!" Venetia happily compromised.

Linked arm in arm, they walked out together.

"I never expected this to happen, even though I've dreamt of seeing Alice more than anything!" she shared honestly turning towards Sophie. Ruby began to explain about her sister and her family falling out, walking beside her.

"Well, I never...." Sophie could not even find the words to express her astonishment properly. Then she said to Ruby: "I have something to ask you." Sophie had a sense of some urgency about her.

"Of course. If I hadn't stayed with you in London, none of this would have happened." Ruby quickly added.

"Being a psychologist, I find it humiliating to admit," she began slowly, "but I suffer from panic attacks. It just came over out of nowhere once and happened a few times ever since. I hate this feeling of panic. I want to run some place, feeling suffocated. How can I better explain it to you? Let's see. It's like when you have no control of what to do and can't even think straight. Once it's passed, it wipes all your energy, leaving you almost paralyzed. Will you please pray for me?"

"I'm sorry to hear it. You've got it. I certainly will pray, Aunt Sophie." Lingering for a moment Ruby added "But what is even better is that you can pray for yourself. Will you consider going to church ?"

"I'll give it some thought," Sophie honestly promised.

Meanwhile, Christian seemed bothered. Ruby made sure to get to the bottom of what was going on with him. She assumed that none of his family turned up. Maybe they could not make it? But he must be pleased at everyone's reaction to his brand new song. Her family already was on its way to the tube.

South Kensington was the tube station they needed for the museum.

The museum greeted them with 18th century masterpieces. The bust of Napoleon and Josephine approvingly towered over all the preserved treasures of humanity here.

Their party moved silently from room to room, only allowing signs of admiration. There was so much art displayed, it would take three life times to properly absorb it all.

Ruby, Alice and Christian sat down on the bench, their legs aching already.

"What do you make of it?" Alice wondered.

Ruby looked at the casts of Moses, David by Michelangelo, and further on at Samson killing a Philistine. "I wonder how much art is biblically inspired. Yet, we are taught in school that life began from one simple, primitive cell leading to produce geniuses like Michelangelo or Antonio Canava, for example. It just doesn't make any sense to me at all."

"Look at the 399 Days by Rachael Kneebone," exclaimed Christian. A massive white, round composition was taking much space in the exhibition hall. A multitude of bodies rose to multiple levels. The modern artist really stood out, but even she could not compete with the replica of the statue of David. He was magnificent, representing a perfect human being, if that was possible. Michelangelo captured the spirit that gave David his title, "a man after God's own heart." How do you go about a task like that from a single block of plain marble? Ruby felt overwhelmed looking at it. Rested, they continued to explore further. The Visitation certainly drew Venetia's attention. While Ruby stood still, intensely studying Elizabeth's aged face and Mary's plain trust in God, she was stirred and encouraged by their faith. Those were extraordinary women, she knew it right there and then. The place was certainly worth a visit.

19

Trent had stayed with John's family for a few days that seemed like months. Every night, once the kids settled down and the heat of the day passed, the grown-ups sat on the veranda sipping on something refreshing, discussing the Scriptures. He figured that he must have existed in a box, not knowing anything about other religion or the Christianity that John embraced. He discovered more in a week than in his thirty years of living. From what he understood, humanity, at every point in history felt a need to worship a higher, of divine origin, being. He learnt that in the Buddhist country of Bhutan the monks had prayer wheels, prayer flags, and prayer chants.

Humans, far removed from civilization, had a deep inbuilt desire, to worship God. When John spoke about God, he sounded like He was his best friend. He was someone he loved deeply and wanted to talk about all the time. His faith felt contagious, without any fear of what people might think. Trent was so moved by it.

The arrival of James could not have been timelier. True, Trent didn't have a home, but somehow he had never felt stronger or at home anywhere else before. He was on a journey, discovering what mattered the most all this time and finally he had arrived. Trent's heart was restless as he headed to the car to meet James.

"Travel safe." John embraced his with much strength.

"Will do."

Hastily saying goodbye to the rest of the family, he headed towards Oaxaca which would take him good few hours. The road was like a rollercoaster, but Trent was used to Mexican roads. The landscape made up for the lack of smooth roads. He could never get enough of the waterfalls and beautiful vegetation, tropical flowers – what a paradise this place really was. As though scales had been lifted off his eyes, he could see that a Creator gave all this beauty to enjoy.

John was right, the Bible made perfect sense. The maze fields, sugar cane fields, corn and agave plantations screamed of abundance. How could he not realize that before? Selfishness is blinding.

Trent sent a text to James: "I'm nearly there. See u soon, Son."

The B & B was easy to find. Trent parked and walked into a spacious hotel. A brown and lanky lad was hanging around. He instantly spotted James, a spitting imagine of him as a teen.

James also noticed him, stunned and unsure what to do for a moment. A range of emotions came and gone. A feeling of incredible warmth washed over Trent. This was his flesh and blood. How could he ever walk away from his son? Not wishing to lose it, he had to pull himself together. The last thing he wanted was to fall apart in public. Everything happened as in slow motion: unable to contain himself any longer, Trent launched forward, embracing James tightly, who let him do it first and responded back. Trent didn't want to let go for a while, scared that this might be just a lovely dream. He could not describe what he felt: a sense of being complete. Not only because he finally was holding onto his boy, but because it felt so right. An incredible peace flooded his heart.

"Hi, Dad!" James broke the silence.

"Hi, Son!"

A simple greeting was the first step to the bridge of their reunion. And before Trent knew, they were standing in front of James's friends. There was no way he could remember all of their names, but they looked like a great bunch of people; sincere, honest, caring. They didn't judge, they somehow understood the significance of this moment. Prior to the fire and before meeting John, he didn't know people like that even existed. So open and willing to go an extra mile to their own inconvenience. On the beach, in the world of surfing, everyone was for himself. On his own. The contrast was mind-blowing. James said his good-byes and Trent helped him with his bags. In the car, alone at last, Trent threw an ice breaker

"So, how is life treating you? Have you had a good time so far? What do you think of Mexico?" True, so many questions were buzzing in circles on his mind. In reality, the only answer he wanted to know was: "Do you forgive me?" But he could not rush James. This boy, mature above his age, waited patiently for him to come around for years. It was Trent's turn to be patient.

"I was invited to interpret for my friends," James was modest about it.

"I didn't know you knew Spanish. I also had to learn myself when I first came. It wasn't easy, but you have advantage of age! How are you with languages?"

"I always hoped that I would come and visit. I have been learning for years now," James braved it up.

Trent looked out of the window, hiding his face from James, but only for a moment, as his eyes had to be on the road.

"Good for you. You take after your mother. I've never been that interested in anything except sports. How is she?" his voice trembled.

"Mum is great. She started to play tennis recently," James chatted the news away, pretending that he didn't notice anything. Even he could sense his father's emotional agony.

Trent became uneasy. A feeling of disappointment swept over him. Everyone eventually moves on. Would she ever forgive him? That was a question he didn't have an answer to. He had to make amends one at a time though.

"Shall we go surfing tomorrow? I'll show you the best spots around here. You'll love it. And the food here is phenomenal. A proper authentic."

As Trent chatted away, James relaxed in his seat a bit. It felt so natural to be with his father. Like they had never even parted. The drive seemed short and the minute they stepped through the door, James was introduced to the family. He got on well with John's family at once. The kids asked him a million questions.

"How do you know so much about Mexico? Even the turtles?" Their minds were spinning fast.

"You can learn a lot from the Internet," James simply pointed out.

The next day the car got loaded early, surf boards waxed and ready for use.

"The Americans must be the friendliest people on earth." He formed his opinion.

"No kidding," Trent agreed wholeheartedly.

"How is your mental endurance?"

"What do you mean? I'm really good at paddling. But it is safer compared to surfing. Just takes a lot of perseverance." James gave his reasoning behind.

"We're not going to surf particularly big waves today. To be able to surf those kinds of waves you have to be able to keep your inner peace. You can't let fear overtake you at any point. I'm sure you'll be good at it," Trent teased him knowingly. "Like father, like son! I don't want to freak you out, but remind me later to tell you about my experience of surfing big waves."

A warm feeling swelled inside James. The hurt that had built up inside him from all those years of separation was disappearing fast.

James could not wait to impress his dad. Water sports came naturally to him. The Carrizalillo Beach was forty minutes' drive away along the picturesque coast. James, looking out of the window, felt the very depth of Mexico in his heart, it's crushing poverty as the milieu to the abundance of dazzling sun, brightly coloured pottery and lush tropical vegetation of the place.

Soon it was time to unpack and get on with the surf. James attached a leash to his foot, and with the board under his arm, followed after his father.

"Look, this is what you do: be prepared to stand, keep your balance, and in the meantime watch the waves. Then, when a good wave is in sight, approach it either on your right or on your left. Let's swim out and you can watch me first, okay?"

"Sure. Sounds good."

"Okay, then."

"Go for it, Dad!"

James sat on the surfboard expectantly while his dad was paddling away. Then quickly standing up, Trent ripped the wave like a pro. It looked dead easy. Not waiting any longer, James got up and started paddling himself. The ocean itself propelled him out. Standing up firmly on the board, he was ready to ride a wave. Before he knew what was happening, a powerful wave picked him and his board right up in the air. As though teasing, it then let go of him, with the board crashing hard on his head. Struggling, James went down, still attached to the board by the leash. Trent appeared out of nowhere, already pulling him up.

"Are you all right?" he shouted, concerned.

"Yes. Just a bit different from paddling, huh?" They burst out laughing. James spit the salty water out.

"Perhaps you need to take a few lessons. I'm rushing you into it. What do you think? I should have told you to always protect your head with your hands. Rule number one."

"It hurts a bit." James touched the top of his head.

"We better get out and have a look."

"All right." Reluctantly, James faced the shore's direction.

Both of them began to paddle to the beach.

There was nothing serious. After a thorough examination and a good sip of water, James was ready to try again. Trent gave a friendly wave to the life guard.

"You possess the true sign of a waterman," Trent reaffirmed. "Even when you're hurt or injured, it doesn't put you off. I think we'll still make a surfer out of you."

Leaving his board, Trent swam alongside James for a while, instructing him how to position himself and how to recognize the right wave. "Paddle, spring up on the board, get positioned. Make sure it's not too forward, not too backwards. Just in the centre. Then catch the wave." The instructions could not be simpler, but doing it was another thing all together. They spent a good few hours just doing that over and over again.

"You're a natural, young man! All you need is some skills. Once you mastered your weight transfer from toe to heel, you'll be ripping like a pro. And always look where you're going," Trent concluded.

"Thanks, Dad!"

"De nada!" A deep contentment washed over Trent.

"By the time to go home, you'll master it. Believe me." James grinned. Every day he Facetimed with Leila, reporting what was happening. His parents began talking as well, usually after he signed off. James was praying that God would move powerfully on his dad's heart. He knew that John's family were praying too. As far as James was concerned, his dad didn't stand a chance. He wondered what would happen first – him learning to surf or his dad becoming a believer.

As a rule, each time they finished their surfing sessions, they stopped on the side of the road for something to eat. A little shack, perched by the side of the road sold most delicious local food. The restaurants back home offered nothing in comparison to the explosion of flavours James was experiencing. A corn tortilla with pulled pork was equal to 50 pence. James enjoyed every moment of it, only missing Ruby. He could see now the allure of this lifestyle pulled you right in, making you forget about the rest of the world. Even though it was painful to admit, he could understand his dad's choices. After satisfying their hunger, James reminded Trent: "What about those big waves, remember you promised to tell me?"

"Once I was surfing a wave that was about the size of a four story building. This mass of water was so powerful that it held me under two waves. My long board snapped. I tore a shoulder tendon. It was the heaviest wipe-out that I'd ever been in. I had to believe that I could outmanoeuvre nature's power. If you don't believe that with every fibre of your being, forget about coming out alive. I kept reliving the moment when I was held under the second wave. For a split second it felt like it was the end, but I kept going. Now, I've realized that this is not the scariest moment at all." Trent took a deep breath, collecting strength. Then continued. "The scariest moment is when God convicts you of your accountability before Him. The Bible teaches that 'it is a scary thing to fall into the hands of the living God.' And the more you dwell on such truth, the more sobering it becomes. I'll have to answer for all those years that I've left you and Mum. I'm truly sorry. I hope one day you would be able to forgive me." Trent fired his wish like a shotgun, scared to hear the answer.

"Of course, Dad. I forgive you." James clasped Trent with all his strength.

To receive forgiveness was not a light thing either, James knew that, feeling his dad sob on his shoulder. He was glad to have a few days to enjoy the new quality in their relationship. On Thursday morning Greg phoned in, explaining that everything was resolved and they are ready to head back. The returned flight was scheduled for Saturday.

At the airport, James and Trent said their goodbyes. "Did you have a good time after all?" Trent affectionately smiled at him.

"Oh, yeah!"

"What about you?"

"Never better."

"I've been thinking a lot. I think I also must head back."

James not anticipating such a radical change of heart, was lost for words.

"I hope I can work things out between me and your mum. I can use all of God's help that I can get."

Overcome with emotion, still unable to speak, James nodded back.

"I want to follow God and let Him lead me in life. I've been looking for meaning in life in the pursuit of self-centred pleasure. It didn't work."

"This is so unreal, Dad!" James finally uttered in a shaky voice. He prayed, he hoped that this would happen. But when it did, he was completely blown away.

"I'll let you know when I'm coming back as soon as I tie up all the loose ends here. Hopefully back for Christmas. How does that sound?"

" Like a perfect plan."

That day he sent a text to Ruby. "How are u? I really miss u. I hope u r not cross with me. How about a catch up time in Bury? Speak soon, J."

The reply came right away. "Miss you too. Lots to tell. Can't wait to see . u soon. R."

James's heart leaped. He read and reread this short text. Soon he would see Ruby. This sounded too good to be true. But first he had a plane to catch.

20

The beginning of November in Suffolk was chilly. James knew that the rate it was going, January would be rather cold. The short time in Mexico with milky blue skies and a warm ocean was a distant memory by now. The only evidence that he had even been there was his still brown skin. Today James was meeting Ruby at the station in Bury St. Edmunds. He was not sure how he survived this long, counting up the days and minutes till Saturday.

Finally, the doors of the train opened up and Ruby stepped out. James's heart did a summersault.

"Hey!" Ruby sent him a friendly welcome.

"Hi! Something is different about you." James could not help observing.

"And you too! I hope I'm more independent now." Ruby was pleased he noticed.

"I think I need to hang out with you a bit longer to give my full diagnose."

"Shall we go to Abbey Gardens for a walk?"

"Sure. Let's go get some hot chocolate. It is so cold."

"Sounds good to me." Walking along Abbey Gate Street, they made a stop at the coffee shop. Then, inhaling the hot aroma rising from the cups, continued on their walk towards the town's ancient walls.

"How was Mexico?" Ruby's curiosity gave in. "I'm sorry for my reaction and for not staying in touch. So much happened and I had to clear my head." Ruby shared with much regret and raw honesty in her voice.

"I let you down, I totally understand. No worries. And how was London?"

"You go first. I can't wait to hear it."

"Okay. Mexico was ridiculously hot. Food was delicious. Learning how to surf was the most exciting part. I also learnt how to play a mariachi tune on a guitar!"

"No way! I'm impressed. I've learned how to control and sustain my voice better. There was so much to learn: how to keep your chin, at what volume to sing, how to reach a good tone, how much air to release. I can't wait to share all my tips with your mum. So, maybe we can have a duet soon?"

"Wow! Sounds almost as complex as surfing. There are techniques for everything. I never thought I'd struggle in the water, but my dad is a good coach." James shared the last fact proudly.

"Go you! I'm so pleased about your dad. But I saved the best news for last. I've run into my estranged sister whilst shopping in Camden Town. Can you imagine that? She reconciled with my parents. We are spending Christmas together!"

"Wow. Epic news! God more than answered all our prayer about our families. It's totally worth trusting Him. My mum and dad have been talking and now spending time together. I think even dad was blown away how forgiveness became possible once she gave it over to God. I'm going to let everyone know publically that I'm a Christian now. Have you thought about being baptised yet?"

"Yes, I have. I'm considering it."

"I dare you to get baptised in the sea!"

"For real? Let's do it."

"My dad and I are going to get baptised together in Brighton on Boxing Day. Andrew is going to do it. He just became a pastor in the evangelical church there. Will your folks come?"

"I'll try to persuade them. Let's hope for a sunny winter's day." Linked arm and arm, James and Ruby entered Abbey Gardens. They had so much to share with each other before they froze to death.

The classical opera concert started at 4 p.m. Armed with knowledge, Ruby listened to singing intently.

"My dream is to control my voice like that one day!" She complimented the singers.

"You will." James could believe anything was possible now.

"Did I tell you about Christian whom I met at At the Round? He says that he's gay." It almost slipped Ruby's mind to tell James about it.

"Oh, really? That can't be easy." James stated the obvious.

"Yes, but think about it. Even if God asks us to give up all the fun and enjoyment to obey Him, isn't it worth it? He did the hardest part for sinners, but we must respond in obedience to Him. Often our sufferings are the biggest encouragement to others. I've heard about it in church. Look at John Bunyan, the author of " The Pilgrim's progress". He was locked in the dungeon with four kids left behind to provide for. His oldest child was blind and his young wife was left alone to look after them. But his book has inspired millions to anticipate an eternity with God."

"At times I try and think about heaven and life with God, but I can't even imagine how good it's going to be. Do you think I would be able to play mariachi like the actor from the Mask of Zorro does on YouTube?"

"Who? Antonio Banderas? I bet you will be able to play guitar better than the guys from Pink Floyd! And I'll sing better than Edith Piaf herself, no tragic lifestyles or harmful addictions there," Ruby remarked with much feeling as though she felt the famous singer's pain. "Whatever God is preparing for His people is going to be unimaginable for now. When I think that my friends or family won't make it there, it makes me truly sad."

"But you can pray harder and trust in the goodness of God." James tried to console her.

"Yup. Can't agree more."

Leila was already waiting for them at the car park.

" My darling! you are so grown since summer. I can't wait to hear about your time in London. What do you make of Suffolk? How was the concert? Sorry, I had to work."

"I'm in love," Ruby said, turning crimson. "With the town, I mean. This quaint town makes time stand still somehow. London is also old, but it is anything but slow." The two were already chatting about singing techniques, being miles away. James didn't mind their catch up one tiny bit.

"You must be freezing. Let's go and get the fire going then," Leila extended an invitation. "You can finally meet James's dad."

Ruby and James sat in the back, sharing their plans about Brighton for Christmas.

Leila listened. How much had changed since this summer!

"We need to make room for all of us to stay. I'm sure Maggie and Andrew are willing to put a few of us up. David and Greg are also coming."

"And Sabine. She is flying over from Mexico. She and Greg are an item," James broke the news.

"It'll be a big party!" Ruby's excitement overflowed.

"The more the merrier. That's why we thought to tell the world about our faith while we're all together."

"God is good," Leila had to add.

21

The remnants of a hundred year old pier were miserably sticking out of a turquoise sea, observing yet another Boxing Day commotion on the sea front. Its black carcass gloomily predicted that such an excitement would pass and everything would go back to monotonous routine. Ignoring the testimony of the pier, that all things will decay some day, the promenade buzzed, exploding from kids' excitement on their new scooters, bikes and ripstiks that cruised along. The grown-ups strolled along, leisurely greeting strangers with a smile, glad for the opportunity to burn off their Christmas indulgence. Mainly

Asian tourists were conspicuous, snapping yet another selfie with the ruins as a backdrop.

James felt like he had lived a hundred years himself. His life had changed: his dad returned from Mexico, his mother willing to forgive his dad, his training with DASCU, meeting Ruby. Considering all these amazing changes, he braved up and invited Phil to the baptism. Phil was genuinely interested and came along. Fear was overrated, James had decided. Once God fills you with courage, the space is taken; fear has no choice, but go.

All the preparations for the baptisms were made in the chaos of the season. Still every guest was housed. A big Boxing Day feast was supplied by Maggie and Andrew. Sabine brought some woolly blankets as gifts from Mexico. They would come in handy today. The air was chilly, but the sun made the day more pleasant.

"Could not wish for better weather, hey?" Andrew cheered everyone on. The sea was so calm. Looking out towards the horizon, Andrew added: "This was not the case in the 1900s when sailors in a boat from HMS Desperate tried to reach the pier. Seven of them tragically drowned."

James recalled the drowning scene in his mind once again. That man's face on Felixstowe Beach would be locked forever in his memory. He glanced in his father's direction, feeling grateful that God gave him another chance.

"Hopefully someone shared the news of salvation with those sailors too," Andrew continued and then spoke about the Ethiopian eunuch and how urgently he wanted to get baptized the minute the Scriptures were explained to him.

"There is nothing magical about baptism," he continued in a booming voice. "You believe and be baptized. You are telling the world that you are not ashamed to be a follower of Christ. He had changed you. Your sins are forgiven. You got a great Saviour because you are a great sinner. That simple. But at the same time following Christ is a very responsible action. You have to really search your heart and see how true your faith is."

All three publicly agreed that they were sinners, ready to follow God as their Master, Lord and Saviour. Trent went under water first. Then James. Then Ruby's turn came.

"I really don't want to get hypothermia or lose my voice." The last grip of fear surfaced.

"You'll be absolutely fine. I don't know one person who died from being baptized. All those who are not baptized should be worried," Pastor Andrew reassured her.

"Okay. I think I can do this." She straightened her shoulders.

Leila had a hot drink and a blanket waiting for her. Ruby took the plunge, letting go of her fears. It felt so liberating. Like someone gave her wings all of a sudden. Coming up from the water, she beamed from ear to ear in spite of the chill. Everyone gathered cheered loudly, drawing the attention of those walking around.

Ruby glanced around with gratitude towards her family. Deep peace washed over her, making her heart bubble with joy. Her life was full of balance. She had peace with God. Still standing on Brighton Beach, in the middle of winter, somehow, she felt transported to another, heavenly dimension. She no longer had to carry her sin alone, the guilt over it was disappearing, like the old pier. At this moment of reflection, Alice came up to her. They hugged, then Alice spoke.

"I can tell this is a very special experience. You're practically glowing. You're a peace maker. God used you to reconcile our family. I'm convinced if it was not for God's intervention, we would never have forgiven one another. And the miracle of it is that He used you. Please never forget that," She encouraged Ruby with much conviction. They walked along the beach for a while, still embracing each other on one side.

Sabine was snapping pictures and filming since John's family didn't wish to miss any details. They could not afford to come, but everyone knew that their thoughts were with them. Trent could never be thankful enough for that fire. Who could've known that first, out of the fire, then by water, God would make him a new man! He simply couldn't imagine such a transformation, proudly looking at his wife and son beside him.

Phil shook James's hand. "Well done, mate. This takes guts. Watch out for bullies now!" They laughed heartily, knowing well how little it takes for someone to bully you.

"If the boy was taking the beating over his shoes, I'll take mockery for God any day. There is a verse in Romans chapter eight, saying: 'If God is for us, who can be against us?' I will have to stand my ground if anyone has a problem with my faith."

"You are so cool, man. Maybe we can look at the Bible together when I come around to play on the Xbox?"

"Any time, mate!" James shook his head, trying to get the water out of his ears. Leaning closer to James, Phil said in a husky voice: "And if DASCU is recruiting, I've started learning Mandarin."

"I'll certainly pass on the message," James assured him. "In fact, I will introduce you to them. Give me a minute please." Still drying off, he searched for Greg and David. Then he spotted Greg, walking off with Sabine, meanwhile David contently chatted with Alice and Ruby. *This can wait*, James decided.

Sabine and Greg left first, rushing to give a hand to the hosts. Maggie assured them that tea would be with all the trimmings because Andrew had never recovered from the years of deprivation whilst on the submarine. He loved to have Christmas pudding first, drenched in rum, then inflamed and served with brandy butter.

That's how life seemed to James. One minute he was bored to go on holiday with his mum, once again, wishing that someone could teach him how to be a real man. Now he was spoilt for choice. His affection was overflowing towards his father who more than made up for his years of absence. He joined the church, willing to volunteer with anything being asked for. Both father and son already signed up for the windsurfing club.

***

On the way back to Andrew's, Ruby and James sat close together in the backseat of Ruby's parent's car. Confident that their quiet voices could not be heard above the music coming from the car radio, the newly-baptized teens were discussing recently happened, miraculous events. James noticed that Ruby grew silent as he gushed with gratitude that his dad was now a believer.

"What about your parents?" he whispered.

"I think mum is coming round. After Alice came back into our lives, I think she is less cynical. God has to convince her that He is the One behind the miracles. She was really listening during the Christmas Day service." Do you think you could ask your church to pray for Mum? Well, for both of them really. I want so much for them to know the Lord like I do."

"Consider it done." James was touched by her concern. Such compassion was a real gift. Inwardly, he prayed that the Lord would develop in him that deep concern for the lost souls that Ruby seemed to have.

***

The table stretched endlessly. Everyone found a chair with a cracker that had their name on it. There were over twenty of them. Andrew gave a blessing and they were urged to start eating while it was hot.

James never felt more complete. He squeezed Ruby's hand under the table. Everyone carried on eating and chatting. They laughed at the cheesy jokes from the Christmas crackers.

His life, with its ups and downs, was in the streamline of God's favour. James had no doubt about it.

ACKNOWLEDGEMENTS

An African proverb says: 'It takes a village to raise a child.' I say - it takes a village to write a book! This novel would never even be born without certain people. So, here it is.

I had been taking creative writing courses for sometime before I met Bridget Whelan at Portslade village. I feel she gave me the wings to write anything I put my mind to. I'm indebted to her for that.

My deepest thanks for Susan Moore, who is not only a perceptive editor, but a deeply spiritual and godly woman with much discernment; your clever insights shaped this story.

Thank you to Leanne Buss, the best friend one can find in Suffolk or beyond. The way your tremendous encouragement, belief in my writing and spare time took my story to another dimension is astonishing.

Thank you to Kelly Spencer for your superb proofreading and both to you and Liz, for constant, much needed cheerleading.

My heartfelt thank you to Sandra Chaplin who made an invaluable contribution to the book at the last minute, but often that is how God provides, teaching us to fully depend on Him in everything. Your sharp observations are astonishing and your obedience to the Lord is contagious.

Don't judge a book by its cover they say! It's certain that everyone will. Larisa, you are a high calibre artist, your design and your meticulousness is jaw dropping. You are a keeper.

The ultimate thank you is owed to my soul mate, a skateboarding champion, a Bible surfer, all time monopoly winner, Stephen. Every time I hear your stories of the past, I think, it can't get more wild, but somehow it does. I appreciate your inspirational walk with the Lord and I'm grateful for letting me have the luxury of writing.

My deep gratitude is for my in-laws, Jan and Ren for being a willing help to spend time with lively grandchildren and for fascinating stories from the Navy times!

And to Ron, a man of incredible encouragement and generosity - the Lord sees your deep love towards His people and so do I.

I dedicate this book to my teens. I pray that you all walk with the Lord and it will become the greatest adventure you can ever imagine. An honest prayer to God changes everything.

Printed in Great Britain
by Amazon